"You know who I am"

Katie thought the voice on the phone seemed far away.

"Come on, sweetheart, don't you recognize my voice? I was sure you'd have guessed by now," the caller chuckled, deep and throaty.

Katie gripped the phone receiver tightly and told herself that this was *not*, was NOT, happening.

"Maybe you're not too happy to hear from me. I bet I know why." The voice became hard now — nasty.

"If I'm 'just a dream' as you put it, then how can I call you on the phone, when you're wide awake?"

Katie listened as if in a trance. Her mind told her it was beyond the realm of reason — but her ears confirmed what she had known all along. It was the guy from her dream. It was Heath!

Katie screamed as loud as she could. And she kept on screaming.

Other Point paperbacks you will enjoy:

The Waitress
by Sinclair Smith

The Hitchhiker
by R. L. Stine

Vampire's Promise
by Caroline B. Cooney

The Dead Game
by A. Bates

The Train
by Diane Hoh

The Ripper
by D. E. Athkins

point

Dream Date

SINCLAIR SMITH

SCHOLASTIC INC.
New York Toronto London Auckland Sydney

ISBN 0-590-46126-5

12 11 10 9 8 7 6 5 4 3 2 1 3 4 5 6 7 8/9

Printed in the U.S.A. 01

First Scholastic printing, March 1993

for Larry Cusumano

Dream Date

Prologue

Katie gazed out her window at the stars shimmering in the sky. There's a saying that when you wish upon a star, your dreams come true, she remembered. Looking up into the sky she spoke her wish aloud. "I'll be seventeen in a few days, and I want my life to be different. I don't want to be quiet Katie — the one guys talk to only when they need homework answers, or a pencil or a piece of paper. I want life to be exciting, and I want a boyfriend who's wonderful. He'll be charming, and gorgeous, and he won't want to spend loads of time with the guys. He'll want to be with me *all* the time.

Katie looked up at the stars and wished as hard as she could.

Be careful what you wish for. You just might get it.

Chapter 1

"Excuse me," Katie mumbled as she maneuvered her way through the sea of bodies to her locker.

"Hey, watch it," a tall girl with long dark hair snapped, clipping Katie in the face with the edge of her hair as she turned.

You watch it, Katie said silently to the offender's back.

Why didn't I open my mouth? she scolded herself.

Because I'm just too tired.

Her answer was partly true. Katie *was* tired.

She was *very* tired.

She'd been awake tossing and turning for most of the night. Insomnia was a condition that plagued her all too frequently.

It was a sneaky little condition, too. It let her alone until Katie almost forgot that she ever had a problem falling asleep — and then it came back. It would visit her for a night or two . . . sometimes three — until she thought she'd go crazy if she didn't get some sleep.

Until she thought she'd never sleep again.

The hours of night that pass before the first light of dawn give you plenty of time to think if you stay awake through all of them, Katie had learned. Plenty of time to brood about where you wanted your life to go — and where it was really going. Katie had done lots of that.

The truth was that being a teenager had not, up to now, turned out exactly as Katie had planned.

She had always thought that as soon as she turned thirteen her life would be transformed somehow — take on a new sparkle. That sparkle would get stronger and stronger every year until her life would be filled with a luminous shimmery light.

It hadn't happened the day she turned thirteen. But that hadn't bothered her much at the time. She assumed that it would happen soon.

But now that she would be turning seventeen tomorrow, she was beginning to worry about that sparkle. What was taking it so long?

After all, there was that saying — "Tomorrow never comes."

Never mind, she told herself. *You just*

moved here — you're in a new school. This is the golden opportunity you've been waiting for — to be the person you've always wanted to be.

But who is that? she wondered.

"Hello there."

The deep, masculine voice made Katie snap to attention. She turned and looked into a pair of incredible deep brown eyes. They almost took her breath away.

It's Jason Miller.

Katie had more than noticed Jason's thick, sandy brown hair, lean, muscular arms, and amazing eyes in the short time she'd been at Warren High. She'd hoped to get to know him . . . very well.

Katie's heart soared . . . then plummeted back to earth and started doing a frantic back-pedal. Now that it seemed like Jason actually wanted to talk to her, everything started whirling around inside. Suddenly all she wanted to do was get away as quickly as possible before he asked her a question and expected her to say something back — before he had a chance to think she was a complete fool because she'd be so tongue-tied and couldn't think of a single thing to say.

"I know you're new here — how do you like

Warren High?" Jason asked, smiling warmly. He was so close, Katie inhaled the fragrance of his shampoo.

"Oh, it smells great," she said, looking into his eyes.

Oh, no — no. I can't believe I just said that. Katie watched a blank, confused look cloud over Jason's features.

"I mean everything is great — just great," she squeaked. "There's my locker — um . . . it's right over there. Uh — 'bye," Katie nodded her head and turned away.

How red is my face? she wondered in agony. *You really blew that one, Katie. If he ever talks to you again, it'll probably be to ask what planet you come from.*

With a sigh of regret she opened her locker and stared in at the books and papers, all lined up neatly and organized perfectly. She started loading books into her bookbag.

"Wow, you must really love to study."

Katie turned toward the voice and saw a girl with black hair and a bright red mouth opening the locker next to hers. She was wearing dangling earrings, a short skirt with an oversized bright red top and wide belt, and the most unusual shoes Katie had ever seen.

"I've been meaning to introduce myself. I'm Raquelle Martinez."

"I'm Katie Shaw." Too startled to feel her usual shyness, Katie continued, "You're in my homeroom — I thought your name was Rachel."

Rachel/Raquelle giggled. "Rachel to the teachers, maybe, but I think I'm really more of a Raquellllle," she said, rolling the last part of her name. "That's what all my friends call me." Raquelle tilted her head to one side and looked at Katie. "So . . . you're new here. Are you getting to know everybody?"

"I guess," Katie shrugged and smiled.

"Listen," Raquelle beamed, "I'm having a get-together on Friday — why don't you come? It'll be nice to have a new face in the crowd."

"Well, sure. Thanks." Katie said automatically.

"Great. Well, I'll be talking to you." Raquelle waved to a guy on the other side of the hall. "Hey, wait up!" Then she was gone in a whirl of color.

Katie felt suddenly self-conscious about her own plain tailored shirt, brown skirt, and sensible beige shoes.

Why did I say I'd go to her house?

Was I crazy?

What will I say to her friends?

Maybe I can say I'm sick. Yes, that's it.

When the time comes . . . I'll say I don't feel well, and I can't go. Katie sighed with relief.

But then she didn't feel so relieved after all.

Wait a minute. What am I doing? she asked herself.

Being the same old Katie.

Being safe.

Being serious.

Never taking a chance.

Katie Shaw, you're going to that party, she told herself, firmly. *You're going, and you'll have a good time.*

Your life is going to change.

Chapter 2

Katie gazed out the school bus window at the steel gray sky. A fine mist of rain drizzled against the glass.

Her bus, Number 11, was barely half full. Katie knew Jason and Raquelle didn't ride Number 11. It was the least-populated route, the one that ended at Ear Howl Creek.

Ear Howl Creek was supposed to be Bear Howl Creek, according to the local story. Somewhere along the line the "B" got lost and it became "Ear." Ear Howl Creek was at the end of the line. The only ones who lived there were Katie and the Tippler twins, Sadie Lou and Melody Ann.

The Tippler twins got stuck in the shallow end of the gene pool, in Katie's opinion. Large, batlike ears stuck out from pointed heads rather too small for their big, graceless bodies. Both had paintbrush haircuts that would've been called "pixies," except that the idea of anything about the Tippler twins being pixieish was ludicrous.

The Tipplers were last off the bus — right after Katie. Though they were her nearest neighbors, Katie had no desire to befriend them, nor were any friendly overtures forthcoming. The twins kept to themselves, and what they lacked in looks they compounded by being thoroughly sly and mean-spirited.

Once, when Katie passed, Sadie Lou had grabbed the edge of her coat and said, out of the blue, "Don't you live in that old house on top of the hill — the one with the fields out back?"

"Yes," Katie had replied, wanting to pull away. Sadie Lou Tippler had eyes as flat as nickles pressed into the round, doughy surface of her face.

"That place has been abandoned for years. They say something awful happened there, and it's haunted." Sadie Lou finished up this last part with a smile full of sneaky satisfaction.

"Don't be ridiculous, only children believe in haunted houses," Katie had told her. After that she had tried harder than ever to avoid the twins.

Katie looked at Sadie Lou and Melody Ann

several seats ahead of her. They were deep in conversation, no doubt exchanging some morbid bit of gossip. Katie sighed. She wished she didn't have to live so far out of town.

Jason and Raquelle lived in the newer section, where the mall was. It was called Greenspring. Greenspring was the official name of the town, now — though everyone persisted in calling the older section and the suburb beyond it, Ear Howl Creek. Why, Katie couldn't understand, since any creek had long since dried up.

Katie had to admit that her house *looked* spooky. Her dad had said it "needed work" — a coat of paint, a fix-up here and there. He said he'd enjoy tinkering around with it.

Then when Katie had seen it for the first time, she thought it looked more like it needed a major demolition and rebuilding from the ground up. The house hadn't been exactly *abandoned*, but no one had lived there for about four years. It looked like nobody had done much with it for several years before that.

The paint was peeling off the outside boards, and one of the shutters was hanging. There were actually *bats* nesting in the attic, and the place was full of spiders.

They'd cleaned the vermin out of the house

and painted, so the inside looked fairly cheery — well — compared to the outside, at least. But late at night, Katie thought she heard noises in the walls.

Her dad said it was just the old building "settling" and there was nothing to worry about. He knew it was structurally sound.

Katie wasn't worried about the soundness of the structure. Try as she might, she couldn't help fearing that there were rats in the walls. That's what it sounded like — scratching.

Sometimes, when Katie was trying to fall asleep, she lay there and imagined the rats scurrying back and forth only inches away. Once she even had a dream like that and woke up screaming, still thrashing at the dozens of rats she imagined swarming over the bedspread. Katie thought she'd never forget the way the rats looked in the dream — their long rat tails, cold, hard eyes, and pointed teeth.

Stop it, Katie, she told herself, leaning back into the seat. *You've never even seen a mouse in that house since it was exterminated. You're just getting carried away with this "spooky house" business.*

As soon as it warmed up enough, her dad would hire some help and start working on the outside of the house. *A new coat of paint and some minor repairs would make all the difference*, Katie told herself. Then things would be blooming and green, and she'd forget all about thinking that the house had ever looked scary.

Katie hoped it was true.

Chapter 3

Sleet and rain, rain and sleet, gloom and doom, Katie thought as she stared out the living room window. The drizzle that had started when she left school had given way to an unrelenting downpour. Hours had passed with no sight of a letup.

Happy birthday to me.

Well, it wasn't exactly her birthday *yet.* She'd been born at exactly one minute past midnight, so technically her birthday was tomorrow.

Katie reached out to stroke Bopper, the elderly basset hound, who was lying next to her on the rug. Bopper stirred and opened her eyes briefly to look at Katie, then went back to dozing.

"I guess you don't feel much like dancing at your age. You'd rather snooze, right, Bopper?" Katie said to the sleepy dog. That Bopper was getting so old worried Katie a lot lately. She couldn't remember when the dog hadn't been there, a constant companion and playmate during all the years she was growing up.

"Ahem!" Katie's dad cleared his throat and rattled the newspaper in a way that said "listen up" as clearly as if he'd spoken.

"Go ahead, Al, we're hanging on your every word," Katie's mother said jokingly.

"Says here, a guy left his job at the post office yesterday afternoon, without so much as a word to anybody — broke into his boss's car — and went tearing down main street doing twenty miles an hour over the speed limit." He paused here, and peered over the newspaper to make sure he had their undivided attention before going on.

"When the cops caught him and asked him why he did it, he said it was because he had *personal* problems. That's right — *personal* problems."

Now he snapped the paper shut and stared at them both, shaking his head. Katie watched her mother look back at him and shake her head exactly the same way, with the same expression on her face.

No need to ask what they're thinking — I know. It's easy.

To either of them, saying any crazy behavior, or even a mildly irresponsible one, was the result of *personal problems* was about the same as saying you were growing a third eye in the middle of your head. That kind of reasoning ranked right up there with deciding you had to do what the voices coming through the metal fillings in your teeth told you to do.

That wasn't the kind of thinking that was practiced in the Shaw family. Oh, no. Here, things were neat and easy to follow. What people were supposed to do was to get on with things, pay their bills, do their homework, keep their clothes clean, smile when they said good morning, wash their hands. People weren't supposed to let personal matters interfere with what was proper.

There were no gray areas, ever. Besides, discussing personal feelings bordered on rudeness. Goodness knows, Katie hadn't discussed anything involving an internal crisis with her parents in years.

Katie looked at them, each settled back into their own reading. They were perfectly suited to each other, always in agreement . . . and it wasn't that they weren't nice, good people. They were.

It was just . . . it was just . . . Katie looked at the living room furnishings. Everything was perfectly symmetrical, perfectly practical. The painting that hung over the couch had been chosen to match the color scheme of the room.

It hadn't bothered Katie much before but lately it was driving her nuts. *I WANT MORE!* her soul cried out. *I want romance . . . and excitement . . . and more, just more.*

Deep inside her, a voice seemed to whisper, *You're going to get it, too.*

The premonition that something big was looming ahead had been growing stronger and stronger all day. Katie strained to get a sense of what it was. Should she run to meet this thing that waited . . . or run the other way?

"Hey, what's going on? You're wearing out the rug." Katie felt her father's voice intrude into her thoughts.

"Oh, just . . . thinking." She hadn't realized she'd been pacing.

"Something on your mind, dear?" her mother asked. "Are you worried about buying some new clothes for school?"

Right, mother. Getting a new wardrobe has been just — preying on my mind.

"No — there's nothing in particular on my mind," Katie lied.

There's everything *on my mind. I know something is going to happen to me soon — something extraordinary. I know it as surely as I know the sun will rise tomorrow, as surely as you'll never mix prints with checks, Mom.*

Katie pressed her hands to her temples. Suddenly she felt very sleepy . . . and strangely off balance.

Steadying herself against a chair, she spoke slowly. "Excuse me, I think I'll skip dinner and try to get some sleep. I'm awfully tired . . . and I think I feel one of those headaches coming on."

Chapter 4

Katie changed into a nightgown and got into bed, pulling the covers close under her chin. She hoped she didn't start hearing any rat noises tonight. She felt so lightheaded.

It must be because I'm so tired.

She prayed that sleep would come soon.

It did. Only moments passed before Katie was floating inside that brief window of space between waking and dreaming.

When she realized she was hearing the noise, she had already been hearing it for some time. It sounded far away at first — but was coming closer and closer.

It's a motorcycle, Katie could tell from the roar of the motor. She'd always loved that sound. It said, Go ahead, break the rules.

Tonight something about that sound compelled her to know more. But she wasn't sure what she hoped to find out.

Who was the driver?

Where they were going?

And then she was outside, standing on her front porch . . . without understanding how she got there. She couldn't remember coming downstairs — and yet here she was. She felt like she was floating a few inches above the ground. Yet she could see that her feet were touching the worn wooden surface of the porch.

Whoever had ridden the motorcycle had parked it already. It stood by the elm tree in front of the house, a huge, menacing black beetle of a machine.

Where was the rider? Katie couldn't see anyone, and she felt her apprehension growing, sending prickles of fear up her spine to the back of her neck.

But what am I afraid of? she wondered.

Then *he* stepped out from behind the tree, out of the shadows, and Katie was so struck by the presence of him that she forgot her fear entirely.

She immediately saw that he was terribly good-looking. His thick, dark hair was windblown from the ride, and he had very dark eyes that made a person feel he saw a lot more with them than just the way somebody looked.

Just a shade above what was considered short, he was extremely muscular.

It wasn't his looks — impressive as they were — that made the impact, though. Katie could tell that much immediately. It was something about him. . . . He was hypnotic.

Now he leaned his back against the tree, looking slightly bored, and measured her up and down with a frank, undisguised stare. His eyes were making her feel very uncomfortable — almost undressed. She was relieved when he decided to speak.

"Hi," he smiled. A twisted half smile that was a little bit wicked — but completely charming.

"Did your motorcycle break down?"

He shifted his weight slightly.

"Nope."

For a moment Katie was at a loss for words.

"Well, why'd you stop?" she said finally.

"I'm looking for something."

"What?"

There was no reply. He just continued to smile at her.

"Where are you from?" she asked, awkwardly.

She had the feeling that he was playing a game with her, and that he knew what the game was, but she didn't.

"What does it matter? I'm here now." He moved away from the tree and came toward Katie. She didn't like the way he moved. There was something slithery about it . . . or maybe it was more like a panther stalking its prey.

"You sure are a pretty girl," he said. This time his smile was so open and friendly that Katie felt herself being charmed all over again. Still, she wanted to be cautious — something about him made her uncomfortable.

Why? she wondered. *Is it just because he's so sexy*?

"You don't know how pretty you are, do you? Oh, I can tell. You keep your nose in a book and you dress real sensible and you're always a *good girl.* That's the way everyone *thinks* you are, but there's a lot more inside.

"Inside you're sick and tired of being little Miss A + and you want something else . . . *but you're not sure what it is.*"

He stared into her eyes. "I can help you find it. And I can help you get it."

Katie felt the touch of his hand on hers through her entire body. His touch was powerful, and pleasant, and threatening at the same time. The blood rushed into her face. Her cheeks were hot.

She pulled her hand away.

"I — I don't even know you!"

"Oh," he said, his voice barely above a whisper. "My name's Heath Granger, Katie, and you're going to get to know me. I already know *you* better than you'd expect — I know you real well."

He took her hand again, and this time Katie didn't pull away.

She didn't even bother to wonder how he knew her name when she hadn't told him.

Everything just *felt* right.

"You know, I feel like I know you, too," she said. "It usually takes a little while to stop feeling shy, especially around guys — but not with you."

Heath nodded with understanding. "You see, Katie, I *knew* you were shy — and do you know what? You don't have to be shy anymore. I'm going to help you find out what a terrific girl you are. I'm going to help you find *yourself*, Katie."

He touched a lock of her hair with a casual motion. "Beautiful hair — beautiful girl. And I like your dress."

And then he vanished . . . into thin air, leaving Katie to think of the *amazing* thing that had *just happened*.

Dress? She panicked suddenly. *I'm* not *wear-*

ing a dress. I've been standing here talking — to a guy I don't even know — and wearing my nightgown.

Only then did Katie's mind voice a loud objection — when she'd gone to bed *only moments ago*, the night was rainy and cold . . . but now the *sun* was *shining* and a warm summer breeze was blowing a lacy white sundress around her legs.

Chapter 5

"C'mon, c'mon Katie, you're going to be late for school!"

Katie jumped bolt upright in bed as her father's voice came crashing into her sleep. She jumped again when she saw the time — seven-fifteen!

How weird. She couldn't remember a time in her life when she'd slept until seven-fifteen . . . even after the worst bout of insomnia.

As she threw on her robe, she was already padding into the bathroom.

It's no wonder I overslept, she couldn't help thinking as she smiled to herself in the mirror. *What a guy. What a dream!*

Too bad it went away so quickly.

A few more dreams like that and I bet I won't have trouble sleeping anymore. Katie laughed a little at her own joke.

She couldn't get over how *refreshed* she felt this morning, and how *especially wide-awake.*

As Katie washed her face she hummed a little song she'd heard on the radio — a happy, rocking tune.

It continued to play in her head as she finished brushing her teeth (*wow, even the toothpaste tastes better today!*) and then went back to her room to dress.

Most mornings, Katie dressed with her mind on automatic pilot. She had enough tailored skirts and shirts so that she could practically get dressed in the dark, and everything would come out all right.

As usual, she started to pull her hair back and fasten it behind her neck with a plain brown clip.

Suddenly, the hand holding the clip stopped in midair.

Beautiful hair, beautiful girl.

She remembered how Heath had looked at her when he said that. How he had touched her hair.

She hesitated.

I've never worn my hair loose before — except to go to sleep.

Why not?

She knew the answer to that one.

I'm afraid I'd feel . . . silly. It's not like I'm the femme fatale *type.*

But then, what type am I? The quiet, serious type?

"Not today," Katie said aloud. Feeling almost daring, she put down the hair clip, and shook out her pale gold hair. Then she "scrunched" it with her fingers to make the curl stand out.

She stared into the mirror. She looked quite different than she did with her hair pulled back severely. Katie *felt* different today, too.

It was only then that she noticed a tiny blue box wrapped in blue paper on her dresser, with a card that said, "Happy Birthday, Katie, from Mom and Dad." She undid the wrapping and pulled a tiny gold chain with a filigree pendant from the box. *Funny, I almost forgot it was my birthday*, she said to herself as she put it on. Katie admired the necklace in the mirror, wondering what she could wear that would set it off.

She remembered a vivid blue sweater dress that her aunt had given her some time ago. Katie had thanked her aunt and put it in her closet, and out of her mind. She had thought the dress was "just not me." But today it *was* her.

* * *

At school, things were different, *too.*

"Hey, hey, hey — who's this here? Can this be Katie Shaw? Where've you been hiding yourself girl?" A guy gave a low whistle as he passed Katie in the hall.

It was Freddy Tappen — known as "Ready Freddy." He was a class clown and class flirt rolled into one, Katie knew.

But he never flirted with me *before.*

"I guess I couldn't hide from you any longer, Freddy," she said with a wink.

Freddie winked back.

I can't believe I'm flirting with a guy! Katie practically clapped her hands with delight.

Not that I'm worried about impressing Ready Freddy anyway, Katie said to herself, surprised at the confidence she felt.

But there was someone else she wanted. Someone she took seriously: Jason Miller, walking down the hallway, coming toward her.

She took a deep breath. "Hi, Jason."

Jason stopped to look at her and almost did a double take. He looked so surprised that Katie almost burst out laughing.

"Well, hi, Katie. You look . . . terrific. Is that a new dress or something?"

"Or something. I just haven't worn it before."

"Well, I'm glad you did. Want me to walk you to homeroom?"

You bet I do!! Thought you'd never ask!! Katie was shouting inside. Her heart was pounding. But all she did was nod slightly and smile. "Sure."

As the day went on, she was more and more convinced that it was the most unusual day of her life.

People who had never noticed her before spoke to her, and Katie answered them back without having to search painfully for words, as she often did. Questions, comments, even snappy comebacks popped into her mind as if by magic. It all got *easier* and *easier.*

What happened? she wondered. *Something is definitely different — and it can't be just because of my hair and my dress.*

It's all so incredible that I should probably pinch myself to see if I'm dreaming.

Something made Katie rein in that thought as it ran through her mind. She turned it over and examined it more closely.

Dreaming. Dreaming, dreaming, dreaming. That's *it.* The *dream.*

Heath said he'd help me . . . find myself.

Katie blushed. *How could I think such a thing?*

She'd never admit to anyone that such a silly thought had entered her mind.

Yet no matter how silly it seemed when Katie *thought* about it, what she *felt* was that she had to see Heath again. *She had to.*

That's why she hurried home from school that day. Her mother, who had come home from work early, heard Katie say something she'd never said before.

"I'm going to take a nap."

"You're *what*?"

"You heard me right. I said I'm going to take a *nap*."

Chapter 6

It wasn't working. It was the first time Katie had ever tried to take a nap . . . and she couldn't even get to sleep at all — let alone have a dream.

After spending twenty minutes alternately staring at the clock and staring at the ceiling, she gave up and went downstairs.

Her mother was curled up on the couch, so absorbed in the book she was reading that she didn't hear a thing as Katie tiptoed over and peered at the title.

"*Love's Raging Passion*," Katie read aloud. "Hey, I'd like some of that."

"OH!" her mother gasped as she looked up with an expression of mingled surprise and guilt. She closed the book and tucked it under a sofa pillow in one quick, furtive motion. "You shouldn't sneak up on people," she snapped.

"Sorry," Katie shrugged. She thought her

mom looked like a little kid caught reading a dirty magazine. What was the big deal about a love story, anyway? It looked more interesting than the stuff her mother usually read — magazines full of recipes and budget tips, or books about gardening.

"It's just as well you came downstairs, Katie, because when you said you were going to take a nap, I was afraid you were sick."

Katie smiled and shook her head. "How come you're home from work so early?"

"I stopped by to check on our vacation reservations, and drop off a check at the travel agency." Katie's mother sighed. "Your father and I are long overdue for a vacation, you know."

Katie nodded.

Eureka! I'll have the place all to myself for a couple of weeks!

"Where are you and dad planning to go?"

"Why, you know, Katie. We'll go to that little resort in Florida where we always go every year." She gave Katie a look that said, *How could that have slipped your mind?*

Every year, Katie echoed to herself. *That's right, why go anywhere else?*

"By the way," Mrs. Shaw opened her purse. What she did next made Katie's jaw hang open.

"Take this credit card and buy yourself some

clothes, dear. Go over to the mall one day after school — and get some shoes, too. You haven't bought anything new in a long time."

Katie took the card with a mixture of joy and disbelief. *Was she suddenly leading a charmed life?*

It's amazing, she thought. *Today, guys flirt with me . . . and now my mother hands over her credit card.*

Is this for real?

"Oh — but dear, buy nice clothes; nothing too wild. I'm the last one to talk against people," Mrs. Shaw paused for a moment to give Katie a slight nod of the head and tilt of an eyebrow. *No gossip, I*, the look said. "But that sweater dress your Aunt Charlotte bought for you is a trifle too . . . clinging."

This is for real, all right. "Okay, Mom."

Katie felt like jumping up and down. Then a thought knocked the wind out of her sails. She had never followed styles very closely, and it just wouldn't do to blow this opportunity and wind up with a closetful of clothes that were all wrong.

She was struck by the thought that only last night, worrying about clothes seemed the most absurd thing in the world . . . and now here she was, *worrying about clothes.*

That's what fashion magazines are for.

"Fashion magazines!" Katie said aloud, startling her mother for the third time that afternoon.

Katie was out the door in seconds and on her way to the drugstore to raid the magazine rack. For the moment, all thoughts of Heath were driven from her mind.

It was much later that night, as Katie pored over fashion magazines, that thoughts of Heath returned.

I really don't think I'd be doing this if it weren't for Heath, Katie secretly admitted to herself as she sat turning pages.

I've never gotten excited about clothes, or even imagined I'd have nerve enough to wear some of the things I'm thinking of buying.

Not that Katie had her eye on anything particularly risqué. It was just that only yesterday she considered anything except a tailored blouse and skirt too daring for her to wear to school . . . but not now.

Be there, Heath, be there in my dreams, Katie prayed as she waited for sleep.

But that night Katie didn't meet Heath in her dreams. That night she dreamed she was in school wearing a new dress that she'd bought.

She thought she looked very glamorous. But as she walked down the hall, people stopped and stared.

"Take off that makeup!" barked a gray-haired teacher, wearing spectacles.

"Who do you think you are?" asked a girl with tiny, piggy eyes.

More and more faces crowded around her. "Where's your brown skirt and sweater, Katie? You used to be such a sensible girl."

"Who told you to wear your hair that way?"

Everyone that walked by looked at her. Two girls in cheerleading uniforms giggled as they passed, and went away whispering to each other.

Katie felt herself redden with embarrassment. Now she was surrounded, the center of a mob of jeering accusers. She turned around and around as comments were hurled from all sides.

"Who do you think you are . . . Prom Queen?" Melody Ann Tippler and her sister Sadie Lou asked, in eerie unison. Derisive laughter followed.

"How could you wear something so clinging?"

"Where's your homework?"

"You should be in the library!"

"Shame on you!"

Katie turned faster and faster, until she was getting dizzy.

The mob had been closing in on Katie — but now they stopped. Something made them all stand still and put their hands to their mouths and gasp as they stared at her with wide frightened eyes.

Her accusers began backing away, murmuring things like, *"Oh, no, no,"* and *"Don't come near me,"* and *"Horrible, horrible."*

When they got far enough away from Katie, they turned their backs on her and ran, shrieking and screaming.

Their sounds of terror reverberated in the empty hallway.

Katie stood alone, facing a wall that was covered with mirrors. She saw her reflection repeat itself dozens of times in the glass.

Again and again, Katie now saw the reason for their fear.

She wasn't wearing the maroon and black outfit she'd put on before she left the house. She was wearing a lacy white sundress . . . except it wasn't white anymore.

Katie was covered with blood from head to toe.

Chapter 7

Heath didn't show up when Katie tried taking a nap the next day after school, even though she was asleep for a full fifteen minutes. He didn't show up in her dream that night, either.

Katie was sad and upset when she thought about Heath, but she was having so much fun in her *real* life that she thought of him less.

Jason Miller had been paying a lot of attention to her. He hadn't asked her out . . . *yet*, but Katie was sure the time would come soon.

After Heath hadn't "shown up" for a couple of days, Katie forgot all about taking a nap and on Thursday afternoon went shopping at the mall with Raquelle.

As they were saying their good-byes Katie began feeling great waves of fatigue washing over her. She knew she wasn't just *tired*. This feeling both coaxed and commanded her, like the pull of an undertow in the tide.

When Katie got home she said she felt a headache coming on and was going to take a nap before dinner. She saw her parents stop reading and exchange glances as she went upstairs — her dad over his newspaper, her mother over her magazine — but they didn't say anything.

Katie was barely able to stay awake long enough to get to her room, where she threw herself on her bed, falling across it as the curtain of sleep swept over her face.

She was standing on the porch again, wearing the white, lacy sundress. She could smell the fragrance from the honeysuckle and rosebushes in the gentle breeze.

What time of day is it? she wondered, and then thought, *Why didn't I bring a watch?* This struck her as absurdly funny and laughter bubbled to her lips.

When she stopped laughing she realized it might be some time in the very early morning, just after sunrise. It was so quiet and still.

Of course it is, Katie said to herself. *I'm in a dream.*

And there he *is.*

Heath was leaning against the elm tree again, wearing the same torn blue jeans and T-shirt with the cutoff sleeves.

“Hi,” he said lazily. But his eyes lit up when he looked at her.

“I’ve been waiting for you,” he said, walking toward her.

As Heath got closer, Katie inhaled the fragrance of something burning. *Had that smell been there before?* she wondered. She couldn’t remember.

What is it exactly? Katie asked herself, trying to recall the odor in her mind.

Was it like burning wood?

Burning leaves?

No — it wasn’t like those things. She’d never smelled this anywhere at all.

Katie wrinkled her nose and drew her shoulders up toward her ears. She didn’t understand it, but something about the odor made her feel afraid.

Was that the way fear smelled?

But then the odor vanished, leaving Katie unsure, doubting that she’d even smelled it at all. Now Heath smelled of a light, spicy fragrance that Katie didn’t recognize, but she thought it smelled better than any men’s cologne she knew of.

Heath took her hand and she felt charged with energy at his touch. He looked down at her with that mischievous, deliciously wicked grin.

"It looks as if there's a whole world right there in those blue, blue eyes of yours . . . Katie blue. I've got a whole world of my own inside, too. What a world it is, if only a girl would prove to me that she really wants to know about it."

Katie looked up at him. "How would I — I mean, how would *she* — prove to you that she really wants to know about your world?"

Heath turned away for a moment. Katie didn't see his lips slide back from his teeth in a smile that was neither mischievous nor charming, *but something very different.*

When he turned to her again, the smile was gone.

"I'm glad you asked that, Katie. I hoped you were interested. People like you and me are *different* from the rest, aren't we? Katie, a lot of girls just don't understand me, and that's why they're not special enough for me."

"What don't they understand?" Katie asked, wondering exactly what Heath meant when he said they were both different from other people.

Of course, with Heath, it was easy to see. He wasn't *real.*

Heath didn't reply, he just stared at her for a moment. His eyes glittered strangely.

Why didn't I notice that before? Katie wondered. It reminded her of the look she'd seen in snakes' eyes at the zoo.

Heath walked a few steps away until he reached the rosebushes at the side of the house. Katie was too shocked to say a word as she watched him rip rose after rose from the bushes.

He seemed to be *attacking* the plants, leaving great, gaping holes where the flowers had been.

What on earth is the matter with him? Katie wondered. *Why is he doing this?*

Heath gathered several roses in his arms. The thorns should have been tearing into his flesh, but Heath seemed oblivious to them.

Katie was stunned when he held the torn stems out to her.

"Here, I brought you some flowers," his face wore a broad smile.

"No — no. The thorns will hurt my hands."

"Hurt?" Heath's smile faded. "Well, have it your way," he said sullenly, tossing the flowers on the ground.

"You shouldn't destroy things, Heath."

"I *shouldn't*?" Heath looked amused. "Well, let me let you in on a little secret, Katie blue. I do a *lot* of things I *shouldn't do*. I'm just a *bad, bad* boy. Are you mad at me?"

Then he gave Katie an innocent little boy

smile that seemed to say, *Forgive me for the flowers. Come on out and play.*

After a moment, Katie had to laugh.

He's teasing me, she thought. *I should have known it all along.*

How could anyone who makes me feel this way be bad? Heath is so handsome, too. He's just a rebel.

"Have you been thinking of me, Katie?" Heath asked suddenly.

"Oh, yes! Every day!" Then Katie told him about all the things that had changed since the first time they had met. But she left out the part about guys flirting with her — especially the part about Jason. She didn't think Heath would appreciate that part.

"It's what I told you, isn't it, Katie?" Heath said when she finished her story. "That I can change your life. Just keep being my special girl."

Heath took both of Katie's hands in his. "My special girl won't try to break up with me, *ever.* And she won't take up with other guys."

Katie felt a twinge of guilt as she thought about Jason. She also had a feeling, (*oh, just a little bit right now*), of being . . . trapped.

She glanced at Heath out of the corner of her eye. He was staring straight ahead. There was something threatening about the hard-set of his jaw.

"I couldn't let my girl cheat on me with other guys. I just wouldn't stand for it."

"What would you do?" Katie asked, trying to control the trembling in her voice.

Heath shrugged and smiled a puppetlike smile.

He's teasing me again, Katie willed herself to believe.

No he's not.

Is.

Not.

Is.

Not.

IS.

"I wouldn't want to break up with you, Heath, or go with another guy," Katie said finally. "But if I did," she continued, feeling impish — daring, "what would you do about it? You're just a dream."

Heath continued to grin, but there was no smile in his voice. "Just a dream, am I? Well, a dream I may be, but not *just* a dream — not at all. I guess I'll have to show you Katie, that I'm much more than *just a dream.*"

Chapter 8

Katie woke up with her head twisted to one side, under the pillow. The first thing she was conscious of was the throbbing pain in her neck. She sat up and turned her head gingerly, with a sharp intake of breath when she turned it too far.

She sat and rubbed her neck in the dark. *Naps are supposed to be refreshing*, she thought. *I've never felt so groggy and discombobulated.* Her head felt as if it were full of smoke, and her stomach was sending distress signals to her brain.

Katie realized that she was ravenous. Her stomach rumbled, and she jumped out of bed, intending to splash some cold water on her face before going down to dinner.

She was halfway through her bedroom door when the phone on her bedside table rang and brought her back. She picked up on the fourth ring, stubbing her toe on the bed frame in the process of hurrying over.

Katie gritted her teeth against the pain for a moment before saying, "Hello?"

"Hi there."

"Who is this?" Katie was more impatient than usual. She was hungry, and had hurt herself in the process of answering this call. She was in no mood to play telephone games.

"You know who I am."

Katie thought the voice seemed far away. *Was it being muffled? Did the caller want to remain in disguise?*

Katie sighed with exasperation. "Listen, I'm not going to play games. Tell me who you are or I'll hang up."

Her stomach gave out with a second, rude, rumble. Her patience was wearing thin, yet starting to give way to a feeling of wariness.

"Come on, sweetheart, don't you recognize my voice?"

Maybe I do — but that's not possible. Katie didn't like the idea that was hovering around the edges of her mind. She tried to push it away.

"Gee, I was sure you'd have guessed by now," the caller chuckled, deep and throaty. "I know *you* real well; in fact, we're getting to know each other better all the time."

Katie didn't say anything. The idea she had tried to push away wouldn't budge. It stood there growing stronger and more frightening, demanding her attention.

"I'll give you a hint . . . *Katie blue eyes.*"

Katie gripped the phone receiver tightly.

Her mind told her it was beyond the realm of reason, but her ears confirmed what she had known all along.

It was Heath!

"Katie? Why don't you speak to me? Aren't you glad I called?"

Katie stood motionless and told herself that this *was not, was NOT*, happening.

"Maybe you aren't too happy to hear from me." Heath's voice had taken on a warning edge.

Katie couldn't speak.

"I thought you'd be glad to hear my voice but I can tell you're not. I bet I know why." The voice had become hard now — nasty.

"If I'm 'just a dream,' as you put it, when you aren't dreaming you can do as you please and I have to stay put. Maybe you could see another guy. Now you think, *He's different, maybe it won't be so easy to fool him.*"

Katie listened as if in a trance. This wasn't the charming Heath she had first met. This was the Heath that had attacked the rosebushes.

What else didn't she know about him . . . yet?

Heath went on. "Let me tell you something. You'd better not think you can lead me on because you won't get away with it. Everything you do and everywhere you go, I'm going to be watching you. All the time. Pretty soon you won't even be able to think a thought without my being there to listen to it."

Katie screamed as loud as she could. And she kept on screaming.

Katie was still screaming several minutes later. She could feel someone shaking her.

"Katie — Katie, wake up! Wake up! You're having a bad dream!"

She was dimly aware that it was her father's voice. She looked at him. "Wake up? I *am* awake!"

Her father shook his head. Katie thought about telling him what had just happened. Then she stared into those clear logical eyes. *No way*, she told herself.

She forced herself to calm down. "I'm okay, now. Really," she said, finally.

Her father rested a hand on her forehead. "No fever. We were a little worried when you didn't come down to dinner . . . but you seemed to be sleeping so peacefully we decided not to wake you."

Dinner? I slept through dinner? She turned to look at the clock. "Four A.M.!"

This has never happened to me before. "I guess I just needed something to eat, that's all." *That's the kind of explanation you can accept, right, Dad?* "I can fix something for myself."

"Okay — but take it easy. Too much food before you go to bed will give you nightmares all over again." Her father turned to leave.

Katie crept downstairs to the kitchen. The clock on the wall grinned like a Cheshire cat, the hands ticking on toward four-thirty.

The question is, Katie said to herself as she fixed a peanut butter sandwich, *was I awake when I got that phone call . . . or not?*

She sat down at the kitchen table and chewed solemnly.

It felt like I was awake. She took a few more quick bites of the sandwich and fed the rest to Bopper, who had magically appeared in the kitchen as soon as the refrigerator door had opened.

If I really was awake, and thought I got a phone call from someone who was in a dream — someone who didn't exist — what would that mean?

The answer was easy.

It would mean she was crazy.

Chapter 9

"Wow, Katie — you look beat!"

"Thanks, Raquelle. I needed that." Katie pulled a book from her locker. She was so weary that the book felt like it weighed fifty pounds. Around her, students shuffled through the hallway on their way to homeroom.

"Well, isn't it just like me to put my foot in my mouth. When will I ever learn?" Raquelle gave an exaggerated shrug. "Maybe you just need some makeup. Uh, oh. I think I just did it again."

"That's okay. I'm sure I *do* look beat. I woke up early and I just couldn't get back to sleep."

That's not the truth. The truth is, I was afraid to go back to sleep because I didn't want to see the guy who might have been waiting for me in my dream.

Katie couldn't think of telling *that* to anyone. She had only been able to write it in her diary.

"Well, cheer up," said Raquelle. "I'm having that get-together after school today. . . . You remembered, right?"

Katie stared. "Oh, no!" she flung a book into her locker with more force than was necessary. "I didn't exactly forget — it just slipped my mind that it was today."

Raquelle shook her head. "Well, unslip it. You can come on home with me right after the last class, since you've never been to my house. We don't want you to start sleepwalking and get lost."

"Ha-ha. Sleepwalking — I get it." Katie put one hand on her hip. "You know, I don't know if I'm really up for anything social," she said after a moment. "I'm so tired, I thought I might just go home and take a nap."

Raquelle looked as if she couldn't believe what she just heard. "A nap! My eighty-year-old grandmother takes naps! Katie, if you're taking naps after school, no wonder your sleep is messed up."

I don't think that's the reason, Katie said to herself.

"You come on over after school and forget about the nap. We'll splash some cold water on your face, you'll put on some makeup, you'll start having fun, and pretty soon you'll forget all about being tired."

"Well," Katie hesitated. Heath would be waiting for her after school. Katie just knew it. He'd be expecting her.

Heath wasn't the kind of boy who liked to be kept waiting.

I want to go to Raquelle's, but maybe I'd better not, Katie told herself. If she did, there might be some unpleasant consequences. Heath was very jealous.

Something might happen.

"Earth to Katie, earth to Katie — are you there?"

Katie gave a little start as Raquelle's voice penetrated her thoughts. "Sorry, Raquelle. Like I said, I'm tired . . . and I guess I'm a little spacey."

"Never mind — listen. You're coming over. End of story. Besides, that's a brand-new dress you're wearing. Isn't there *somebody* you want to get a good long look at you in it?"

Just then Katie saw Jason Miller out of the corner of her eye. *Somebody* was heading her way.

"Morning, ladies." Jason stopped in front of Katie and leaned one hand against the locker, holding his books on his other hip. He stood close to her — closer than he had to.

"So — you're coming over to Raquelle's house later, aren't you?"

"I invited her," Raquelle interrupted, "but she's playing hard to get."

"Well, then, let's start convincing her," Jason smiled into Katie's eyes. The closeness of him was making her heart beat faster. She laughed quickly.

She didn't feel the least bit tired anymore. "Okay, okay, I'm going, already."

Jason tapped her lightly on the arm. "All right! That's the spirit! See you there." Katie stood watching him walk away.

"Well!" Raquelle said after a moment. "Should I feel slighted because he convinced you a whole lot quicker than I did?" She shot Katie a meaningful glance.

"Am I that obvious?"

Raquelle grinned. "Well, let's just say *I* could tell there was something going on there. But don't panic, he was interested in doing some convincing, wasn't he? Hey — he doesn't get that close when he wants to ask *me* the homework assignment."

"Well, that's a relief." They started toward homeroom.

The dream with Heath Granger in it seemed far away and unimportant now. Katie could hardly believe that only moments ago, the thought of Heath had so filled her with fear that she had almost turned down a chance to get to know Jason Miller.

Honestly, she said to herself. *He* is *just a dream, and why should I be scared of a silly old dream?*

Chapter 10

I wouldn't have missed going to Raquelle's this afternoon for the world, Katie said to herself as she eased into the shower later that evening. She shivered a little as she waited for the water to warm up. Soon the shower stall was clouded with steam.

Katie grabbed a bottle of new, scented shampoo she'd bought and lathered up her hair.

Funny how I was always shy around new people but this afternoon everything was fine. I never had so much fun. Of course, Jason was the best part.

Katie remembered how Raquelle wanted to show off her new CD player, so she'd brought it into the den where everybody was gathered, and turned on the music. She'd been trying to get people to dance, but the situation looked pretty hopeless. It was the familiar routine of the guys standing on one side of the room and the girls on the other.

Then Jason had crossed the room, had come over to her and smiled. "Wanna dance?"

And just like that — they'd started dancing. Soon everybody else followed.

This water is getting too hot! Darn this old-fashioned plumbing! Katie resented having her happy memory interrupted. *I didn't touch the knobs, so why is the water heating up?* Katie turned on more cold water and went back to remembering.

She and Jason had danced and danced. Finally, when they both thought they would die of thirst, they went to the kitchen to get something to drink.

"Let's just stay and talk for a while," Jason said, leaning up against the sink. "I've been hoping for a chance to get to know you and this is the first moment we've had alone. So — tell me about yourself."

"What would you like to know?" Katie asked, teasingly.

"Anything and everything." Jason fixed her with his clear gaze.

Katie's old self-consciousness returned, but only for a moment. "Well, I used to be sort of quiet, you know," she said, looking down at her hands. "I had friends and all, but I was just — quiet . . . serious. It's different here. It's almost like I'm somebody else."

Katie looked at Jason sharply to see if he seemed to think that what she said sounded strange, but he was simply nodding as if he was listening carefully. "I can be kind of quiet myself sometimes, and then the next minute — you can't shut me up!" He laughed a little.

Katie thought he had a wonderful laugh. "Sometimes I still think I'm supposed to be serious all the time," Katie told him.

Then — and Katie's heart beat faster, just thinking about it — Jason had smiled at her and said, "Oh, I bet you don't give yourself enough credit. You know, you may *be* sensible and serious, but that's not the way I'd describe that dress you're wearing. And that's not the way it makes me feel."

He gave her an impish grin as he moved closer and took her hand . . .

Not again! Hot, hot water gushed out of the showerhead so suddenly that it nearly burned Katie before she could get away from it. She stepped out of the scalding stream, reached around it, and turned the cold water on full force this time. *What is going on? Is the whole plumbing system in this house breaking down completely? It's acting like it has a mind of its own.*

Now, Jason, where were we when we were so rudely interrupted?

"Why don't I take you home?" he had asked. Katie nodded, and that's when "Ready Freddy" had stumbled through the kitchen door.

Jason had straightened up and eyed him critically. "Hey, man — have you been drinking beer . . . lots of beer?"

"You bet I have." Freddy grinned a wide, clownish smile.

"Smells like it," Jason snorted. "Where'd you get it?"

"You want some, pal? It's out back in my car."

"In your car? You're drinking beer and you're driving? Oh, that's perfect, Freddy. Just perfect."

"Somethin' wrong?" Freddy asked, weaving a little.

"Yeah. Really, Freddy, you're my friend and all, but you can be a real jerk sometimes. There's no way you're driving in the shape you're in. I'll give you a ride."

Freddy opened his mouth to say something, but apparently forgot what it was. His jaw hung open for a moment before he remembered to close it.

Jason shook his head. "C'mon, Freddy — just wait for me outside." He gave Freddy a light shove out the door.

Then he turned to Katie. "I'm sorry. I've got to drive Freddy home. We promised we'd look out for each other when it came to situations like this — although right now I feel more like running over him than taking care of him."

"I think it's nice that you take care of your friends," Katie told him. The fact that Jason was taking Freddy home had made him seem even more romantic — if that was possible. Especially since the next thing he had done was to ask her for a date for Saturday night.

"I've got a date with Jason Miller for Saturday night!" Katie sang out loud.

Something is wrong, she realized suddenly. *Very wrong.*

The water was hot . . . and still getting hotter.

It was *much too* hot.

It happened so fast that Katie *felt* the heat before she was *conscious* that she felt it.

Warning signals were flashing in her brain. Katie made a frantic grab at the cold water knob. *I know I turned this thing as far as it would go.*

Katie gripped the knob tightly and *turned.*

The knob spun crazily in her hands, around and around and around. *It's broken!*

The warning signals were so loud now that Katie couldn't think through them. She was starting to panic.

She still had the presence of mind to give the showerhead a shove to deflect the scalding stream of water toward the wall and grab the handle on the glass door.

Katie's hands were wet and soapy, and in her panic, her fingers kept sliding off of the handle. She couldn't get a grip on it to let herself out.

That's when her presence of mind left her. Her thoughts raced in circles like an animal that knows it's trapped. *I've got to get out of here. I've got to get out of here.*

The steam was so thick she couldn't see her hand in front of her and the water was so hot it was burning the soles of her feet as it ran toward the drain.

Katie lost her balance and fell on one knee, catching herself with her hands just in time to avoid cracking her head on the tile.

The combined pain in her knee and her hands, where they rested in the scalding water, made her feel sick as she pushed herself to her feet. She knew that even if she were able to break the glass door to get out — her cuts and gashes would be terrible.

A vision of the bathroom with blood and broken glass everywhere clicked into her mind for a shutter-speed fraction of a second.

Then her hand had rested on the *washcloth.* Something in her brain forced her to look at it and pay attention.

Katie understood what she had to do. Fighting to keep calm, she used the washcloth to give her hands the traction she needed to grip the handle. Now she turned it easily and stepped out of the stall.

She leaned against the basin, feeling dazed. Steam billowed around her. She cracked the bathroom door open to let it out.

Finally, she took her terry cloth robe from the hook on the door and put it on. Then she wrapped a towel around her hair.

She glanced at her reflection in the mirror and saw her eyes wide with fear in her pale face . . . but only for a moment. Because then she saw something else. Written in the steam on the bathroom mirror was a message . . .

WAITING MAKES ME VERY ANGRY

Chapter 11

The terrifying message in the mirror burned into Katie's brain as her senses wrestled with one another. Her mind refused to accept what she saw, but no matter how hard it tried, it could not erase the words that remained before her eyes.

I must be losing my mind, Katie said to herself. *That's the only explanation.*

Is that the worst thing that could happen?

If I'm not losing my mind, then what's happening is real.

Then Katie couldn't stand it anymore. Unmindful of the pain in her knee, she ran to her bedroom and hid under the covers, shaking like a frightened child. Her teeth chattered. Her eyes darted around the room.

Heath is here in the house. I know it. I can feel it, Katie said to herself. *He's curled up and hiding here somewhere.*

Watching.

Waiting.

Biding his time.

Katie wrapped the sheets tightly around her and backed up against the headboard.

But soon her *need to know* won out over her fear and Katie got out of bed and started down the hall to the bathroom. She could hear the steady rain of water as she got nearer and remembered she had left the shower on.

The steam in the bathroom had evaporated.

There was no trace of any message on the mirror. *None.*

Katie opened the door of the shower stall and ran her fingers cautiously under the spray. It was lukewarm — *maybe not even that hot.*

I know I wasn't imagining things, Katie told herself as she turned the water off. When she nearly fell asleep standing up in the bathroom, Katie went back to her bed and soon drifted into a restless slumber.

Katie had not even fully entered the dream when she saw Heath, as if from far away, pacing back and forth, waiting for her. As soon as he caught sight of her he rushed toward her.

Heath wasn't smiling.

"What's the idea of making me wait? I thought we had an understanding." Heath was so angry he nearly glowed red.

"Not after that phone call," Katie said. She was determined to stand her ground. "Just who do you think you are, scaring me like that at four o'clock in the morning?"

She stared Heath in the eye.

"Your little love note in the bathroom wasn't appreciated either. I could've been covered with blisters — or worse."

Her tone caught Heath off guard. He hadn't expected her to come back at him. He looked confused for a moment. Then his approach changed — chameleonlike.

"I'm sorry, Katie. I wanted to see you, and I thought you'd be here if you wanted to see me. That's why I wrote the message, but I didn't mean for the water to be so hot it would hurt you. I'd never hurt you — honest." The sharp edge in his voice had given in to honeyed pleading.

"Well, it's not that easy, Heath. You can't just erase the whole thing." Katie folded her arms stiffly. She was put off with this waffling of moods.

But Heath kept looking at her with such misery and sincere remorse that Katie felt herself relenting.

"Don't do anything like that again, Heath, and I mean it."

I know I shouldn't forgive him but I just can't help it somehow.

"I won't Katie — I'm sorry. I'm so sorry."

"I forgive you," Katie found herself saying, even as she wondered why.

Then Heath took her in his arms. With Katie's head pressed against his chest, the triumph shone unguarded in his eyes.

"Why do you just wait for me?" Katie murmured, looking up at Heath.

Heath laughed. "I'm a dream, Katie. Somebody's got to dream me up."

"You mean, if I don't dream you, you don't exist?"

"It's not that I don't exist, but, it's sort of like a book. It can be there on the shelf all the time, but unless somebody takes it off the shelf and reads it, nothing happens. The more you 'read me' the more I 'happen.' "

Katie nodded. She felt a little sorry for Heath, though it was hard to feel sorry for a guy who looked so handsome, and was so wild. *Not to mention unpredictable.*

Suddenly Katie shoved Heath away. Backing up, she crossed her arms in front of her chest and glared at him suspiciously. "How much can you see?"

Heath looked at her blankly. "See what?"

"Stop it," Katie snapped. "You know what I mean. Can you see through my dress? Can you see me in the shower? What special powers do 'dreams' have?"

Heath's face assumed a slow, suggestive grin.

"I'll never speak to you again, you slimy rat." Katie began running away from Heath.

"I'm not coming to see you ever again," she called back as she ran. "I don't care if I have to stay awake *forever*."

Suddenly he was beside her. "Wait, Katie, please — I'm sorry. I was only teasing." The words tumbled out as they ran. "I can't see through your dress, and I didn't see anything in the shower. I promise."

Katie stopped and faced him.

"How did you know where I was when I was in the shower . . . and how did you write the message?"

Heath didn't say anything.

"Well?" Katie pressed her advantage.

Heath leaned against a tree and pressed his lips into a thin line. When he spoke, the words came slowly, as if he were choosing them very carefully.

"It's not like seeing with your eyes. I *know* things. I can *sense* things. I get a *feeling* about a person."

As he spoke and Katie listened, she could feel her anger draining away once more. *Why is it so hard for me to stay angry with him?* she asked herself.

Because he still has me hypnotized.

Heath leaned closer to Katie, and she felt his arms encircle her. "Don't be angry with me, Katie," she heard him murmur into her hair. "I want to be with you so much. *And I want you to be with me all the time.*"

Chapter 12

"Come down here, Katie! I won't stand for you sleeping all day long!" Katie felt her father's voice slice into her sleep. He always seemed to be yelling at her to get up these days.

Katie turned on her side and pulled the covers up over her head. *Really*, she thought, little pins of irritation forming behind her eyes, *nobody ever lets me get any sleep anymore.*

Moments later there was a loud knock at her door. "This is ridiculous, Katie. Get up at once." It was her mother's voice.

"Let me alone — it's Saturday," Katie protested. "Who are you, the sleep police?" she muttered under her breath as she buried her face in the pillow.

"If you're not out of bed in five minutes then you're too tired to go out tonight!" her father's voice boomed.

"Okay, okay. I didn't know it was so late," Katie said wearily, putting both feet on the floor.

She didn't want to break her date with Jason, but she wasn't looking forward to it as much as she had been — before last night. Now she felt a little disloyal, and a little guilty, about going out with him. *And a little scared.*

It had been wonderful being with Heath — at first. *But now I'm not so sure I want to be Heath's special girl,* Katie thought to herself. *I don't think I want to be with him all the time.*

Katie pulled on jeans and an oversized sweatshirt. She decided she didn't want anything to interfere with her date with Jason tonight — *including Heath.*

Bopper lay dozing in a corner of her room. The basset hound gave a tiny shake of her head as she slept.

What do dogs dream about? Katie wondered. The thought sent a chill down her spine. *Would Heath take his jealousy out on a helpless old dog?*

Heath was charming . . . but there was something very scary about him. Katie wasn't sure just how much he was capable of when he was angry.

Come on, Katie, this kind of thinking is getting out of control, she told herself. *You don't really take this dream guy stuff seriously, do you?*

The basset hound made little yelping sounds in her sleep. She was "running" sideways on the floor with her feet.

Katie stared. *No, it can't be.*

The "running" turned into violent thrashing motions.

It's like she's trying to get away from something. Or someone, Katie thought, gritting her teeth. She tried shaking the dog, but the basset hound continued to sleep.

"Bopper, wake up!" Katie's insides were starting to churn. She didn't know what she'd do if something happened to the dog.

Heath, if you're there, don't hurt her, please don't hurt her.

Bopper had always been a quiet sleeper. Now her yelps were turning into howls. Katie felt as if a hand had just reached in and grabbed her heart.

The old basset hound was slowing down. Her feet weren't thrashing nearly so fast.

Katie shook her again. There was no response. She lifted one of the dog's eyelids.

Then Katie backed away and she pressed

the heel of her hand to her mouth.

The dog's eyes had rolled back in her head.

Katie watched as Bopper stopped making the motions with her feet, gave a single sharp yelp, and was still.

Chapter 13

"I've never seen a dog move or make noise like that when it was sleeping. Bopper is usually quiet, and it scared me half to death," Katie told Jason.

Jason smiled at Katie across the table. "I'm glad it was a false alarm — that your dog's okay. My collie yaps in his sleep all the time — makes all kinds of racket — then goes back to snoozing peacefully. I think it's a riot — unless it wakes me up."

Katie nodded. She was impressed that Jason had decided to take her out to dinner. It was a *real* restaurant, too, not like the kind of places she'd been on dates with other boys — pizzerias and hamburger joints. She hoped that Jason didn't think she was the kind of girl who believed money was all that counted.

"I hope you don't think I'm trying to show off by bringing you to a place like this," Jason said, as if he could read Katie's thoughts. "I usually do something more casual on a first date but I got some extra money for my birthday. I wanted this date to be perfect, so I said to myself, 'Why not?' "

Katie smiled, amazed that he was so tuned in to her thinking. When he reached across the table and took her hand, she was conscious of how gentle his touch was. Though his hands were large and strong, there was nothing rough about them.

Jason doesn't make a big deal about being tough, or strong, the way Heath does, Katie thought to herself. *Yet it's obvious that he's both.*

It's such a relief to be with someone who's not always acting mysterious, or like some kind of character in a movie . . . someone who doesn't have anything to hide.

Jason seemed so *normal.*

What would you think if you knew that this afternoon I was nearly hysterical because I thought a guy from my dream was trying to hurt my dog? Katie wondered as she looked at him.

The evening passed by so quickly, and was over much too soon. "Where on earth did the time go?" Katie asked as they sat in Jason's car in front of her house.

"Thank you for a terrific time." Katie looked at Jason, her eyes shining.

Jason tapped his hands on the steering wheel. "I wanted tonight to be perfect, and it was. More than I could have ever imagined."

Katie blushed in the dark. She was glad the curtains were drawn and the lights were out in the house. That meant her parents were asleep.

She wanted Jason to kiss her — and she didn't want anyone staring at them.

When Jason didn't move toward her, Katie felt a pang of disappointment. *I guess I should just get out of the car,* she thought, *and not make a fool of myself.*

"Well, good night." Katie fumbled for the door handle.

"Wait — " Jason reached across her body and put his hand over hers. "Don't leave yet."

"All right." Katie let go of the door handle. Jason removed his hand from hers, and Katie put her hands in her lap.

"I've just been composing a poem for you. It's a sort of love letter. . . . Ready?" he asked with a grin.

Katie looked down into her lap, letting her gold curls fall and partly cover her face. "You're embarrassing me," she laughed.

"Come on, I'm the one taking the big risk

here," Jason said laughing. "Well, here goes.

A rose is beautiful
So are diamonds and pearls
Katie Shaw
Would you be my girl?

"Well, what do you think?" he asked. "If I'm not a prizewinning poet, it's the thought that counts."

"Oh, I like the thought, Jason," Katie said softly. "Of course I'll be your girl."

Jason leaned toward Katie and placed his hand under her chin. He tilted her face up to his.

Her heart fluttered gently and his arms slipped around her. She closed her eyes and waited for the kiss . . .

OH BABYBABYBABY
TONIGHT'S NEWS UPDATE SEES
WAWAWAWAWAWAWAWANNA

The radio blared suddenly from out of nowhere, causing them both to jump as it switched crazily from station to station. Katie held her hands over her ears while Jason fumbled with the radio dials.

No matter what knobs he turned, the radio

continued to blare its chaotic sounds.

Next the windshield wipers began to swish and the lights began blinking off and on.

Katie's every muscle tensed. *I know it's Heath,* she thought, clenching her teeth. *I know he's here.*

The car began to rock, pitching unsteadily back and forth as the horn set up a persistent wail.

Now the car alarm went off, adding its own hideous and insistent bleating to the cacophony of noise.

Something under the hood was starting to smoke.

"I can't turn this crazy thing off!" Jason yelled, wrestling with the ignition key.

Katie watched as the lights in her house switched on, one by one.

"I've got to go," she shook her head helplessly. "My parents are awake."

Jason nodded, looking at her with what she hoped was understanding.

Quickly, Katie stepped out of the car. She wasn't even halfway up the walk when the car stopped moving. Then the windshield wipers were still — the radio and other noises silenced.

I know why, too, Katie thought as she blew a kiss to Jason.

Chapter 14

The dream came rushing in to claim Katie as soon as she closed her eyes. It whirled around her until she was pulled completely into its world. Soon she was standing on the porch in the sunshine. Heath was glaring at her. She could feel the heat of his rage all the way from where he stood in the yard.

"Just what was going on tonight?" he called out.

Katie descended the porch steps and walked toward Heath. Stopping directly in front of him, she gave him a cool, defiant stare.

"You'd better explain what you mean."

"It's simple," Heath snarled. "What I mean is: Where did you go tonight, with whom, and what did you do?"

"It's none of your business." Katie turned her back on Heath, dismissing him.

"I asked you something," Heath said, "and I expect you to give me an answer. . . . Now." His voice was so hard and flinty, Katie felt as if rocks were being pelted at her back.

She whirled around in surprise. *He always backed down before. What's going on now*?

Heath looked particularly sinister tonight as he stood under the tree in Katie's yard. Something about the way he looked at her made Katie fear what would happen if she told the truth. And at the same time, she was afraid of what would happen if she lied.

"Well?" Heath prompted.

"I — I went out with a friend."

"Friend?" Heath smiled an eerie, pasted-on smile. "I hadn't thought about it, but I don't know much about your friends, do I? I'd like to start learning," he said with mock enthusiasm.

Heath began walking in a circle around Katie. "Let's start with the friend you met tonight. Tell me about that friend." Heath kept making the circle smaller and tighter.

Katie stood still and silent, feeling as if she were an animal caught in a snarling circle of wolves. One wrong move and the wolves would pounce and tear her to pieces.

"TELL ME ABOUT THE FRIEND YOU

MET TONIGHT, KATIE. TELL ME ABOUT *HIM*." The words hissed out like steam from a radiator.

Katie's breath caught in her throat.

"Wonder how I know it wasn't a girlfriend, don't you?" Heath said with a smirk. "I could feel the atmosphere in that car. Things were really heating up in there, weren't they? You forgot all about me."

Katie covered her face with her hands.

Now Heath's voice whined. "I thought I could count on you, Katie." He sounded small and sad and alone. "I guess I shouldn't expect a girl like you to care about someone like me."

Katie dropped her hands. She looked at Heath sitting slumped on the porch steps.

Suddenly it struck her that Heath played three characters: Mr. Wonderful (incorporating Mr. Mysterious and Mr. Tough Guy), Mr. McNasty, and The Poor Little Boy.

Why did it take me so long to see through his routine?

First I get bullied by Mr. McNasty, then I'm supposed to feel sorry for The Poor Little Boy and let him have his own way. And if I'm lucky, Mr. Wonderful (definitely the best of the three) will come out and play.

Now that she understood it, Katie couldn't believe she had ever fallen for Heath's manipulations. The hypnotic spell was definitely broken.

Heath just doesn't know it yet, Katie thought to herself.

Heath was still pouting, and he was starting to wonder what was taking her so long, Katie could tell. Every so often he would drag down the corners of his mouth a little more and glance at her out of the corner of his eye to see if she was making a move.

Careful, Katie. He's a mean one, and it looks like you're trapped here with him.

"Come on, Heath, let's just go for a walk." Katie carefully kept the contempt she felt out of her voice.

Heath looked up, a little startled. After a moment he stood up and nodded.

You were expecting to be fussed over quite a bit more, weren't you, Heath? But you've decided to settle for this.

They walked toward the road that ran alongside Katie's house. Heath picked some white clover and handed it to Katie.

Mr. Wonderful decided he'd better make an appearance.

"Come on, let's cross to the other side of the road," Katie said suddenly as they were nearing it. "I've never explored over there, and when I'm awake it's cold and awful."

"Nah — it's nicer over here. I've seen what's there already."

"Well, then you can show me," Katie coaxed as she tugged at his sleeve.

He pulled away. "Stop it, Katie. I told you I don't want to go."

Uh, oh. Pretty soon Mr. McNasty is going to be back.

Katie felt the back of her neck prickling. *Why does everything have to be* his *way all of the time?* She felt herself getting angry in spite of her effort to stop it.

"Don't be a party pooper, Heath." Katie hoped her smile looked natural. She dashed into the road. "I want to see what these woods are like. If I'm in a dreamworld, I want to see it!"

Then Katie started to run.

"Katie, you're not going over there!" Heath bellowed.

It's Mr. McNasty all right, Katie thought as she ran. She kept on running.

He'll follow me, she thought. *Why is he being such a stick-in-the-mud*?

But when Katie got to the other side of the road and turned around, Heath wasn't following her at all. He wasn't even there.

Then none of the dream was there — it vanished, leaving only darkness.

Chapter 15

Katie's eyes snapped open.

What a strange feeling. It's almost the way you feel when you lose your balance and catch yourself just in time — before you hit the ground, Katie thought as she sat up in bed.

The same sensation had kept coming and going all day Sunday. She had kept to herself all day, unable to do anything but go over the dream again and again in her mind. Yet this morning something compelled her to review what happened one more time. Katie tilted her head back and remembered.

Just after she had crossed to the other side of the road she had felt herself falling. The dream had vanished, and there was only darkness. She had kept falling a while longer — and then she was awake.

Katie sighed. *I know there is something im-*

portant about what happened. If only I could figure out what it is.

She was suddenly aware that the alarm had been clanging away.

Oh, no! I've overslept again! Katie said to herself as she looked at the time.

Today I'll be late for sure.

She ran to the bathroom, washed her face and brushed her teeth in record time.

Thank goodness I laid my clothes out last night. Katie hurriedly threw on a soft burgundy angora turtleneck and pulled on her short black skirt.

As she clattered downstairs she could see her father's tight-lipped expression. She tried to make herself as small as possible as she slid into her seat.

"I know you had trouble sleeping in the past, but now you're sleeping way too much. You're ignoring the alarm in the morning. Is there no middle ground?" Her father asked in an impatient tone.

"I don't think I'm sleeping too much," Katie protested.

"Oh? Well, think again!" her father thundered back. "And all day yesterday you acted like you were in another world!"

Katie's mother sat in silence, looking at her

quizzically. "Do you want to see a doctor?" she said, finally.

Maybe, but not the kind of doctor you have in mind, Mom. Katie shook her head and stared into her orange juice.

"I've been staying up late studying. This is a new school and I want to make sure I . . . adjust to their teaching methods." *I hope that sounds good,* Katie prayed.

Her parents were nodding with approval.

"I've got to go." Katie jumped up suddenly, snatching a piece of toast and pulling her coat on. She grabbed her books and waved good-bye as fast as she could. She didn't want them to think of any questions to ask.

As Katie ran down the drive and headed toward the bus stop, she realized that the whole breakfast table conversation had upset her enough that she didn't want the toast anymore. Looking guiltily around, she threw it into a ditch at the side of the road.

At the bus stop, Katie deeply inhaled the crisp, early spring air. *Could I imagine the way this place looks in the summer vividly enough to dream it?* she wondered.

In her mind's eye she painted the leaves on the trees and the flowers on the bushes. She could smell the fragrance of the honeysuckle and the roses and the grass, and she could hear the song of birds.

Three sharp honks of a horn blasted the morning suddenly back into focus. The bus stood in front of Katie, and the door was open.

"You joining us for the ride this morning, Katie?" asked Biff, the round-faced bus driver, with a smile.

Katie blinked a few times.

"Sure, sure I am," she said sullenly, climbing aboard the bus.

Biff chuckled.

"Looks like you went back to bed there for a minute. When I was driving up I coulda' sworn you were asleep on your feet. Just takin' yourself a little snooze. Heh, heh, heh."

Biff's merry expression faded as Katie glared at him. "I wasn't 'taking myself a little snooze,' at all, as you mistakenly suggest."

As Katie turned and flounced into her seat, the Tippler twins exchanged meaningful glances. "What are you looking at?" Katie snapped, making them recoil in shock and surprise.

I should have taken the car, Katie thought as she threw herself into her seat. *Imagine saying I was "taking myself a little snooze." The nerve. Why is everyone suddenly so interested in whether I'm sleeping or not?*

But as the ride went on, Katie's thoughts gradually changed.

How could I have been so rude to Biff? How could I have been so mean? What on earth is the matter with me?

Oh, you know what the matter is, all right, Katie. You don't want to believe you dozed off at the bus stop. But you probably did. Why would Biff make it up?

"I'm sorry I snapped at you, Biff," Katie said quickly as she prepared to leave the bus. "I guess I'm just tired."

"No problem," Biff said, giving Katie a smile that told her the matter was instantly forgotten.

Still, she felt guilty as she trudged into school.

Katie's mood brightened when Jason fell into step with her in the hall.

"How about that old car Saturday night, huh?" Jason asked with a grin. "That old bomb — it's never had so much energy. I think it's got the equivalent of losing your marbles." Jason tapped his head with his index finger.

"No more trouble on the way home?" Katie asked.

"Not a bit. I'm going to check it out, but there was no problem when I drove home. Look — I've got to go to a class early —

maybe we can get together later?"

"Oh, I don't know if that's really a good idea," Katie hesitated. "I mean, there's homework and all."

And of course that special guy waiting for me in my dreams. My own worst nightmare.

"You sure?" Jason looked at Katie with a mischievous smile. "Come on with that homework stuff, Katie. From what I know about you, I'd guess you've done all your homework from now to the end of the month. Are you sure you're not just playing hard to get? If you are, it won't do you any good, because I'm going to be very persistent."

"Okay, okay. I get the point," Katie laughed. "You know very well I'd like to see you later."

"Great." Jason gave Katie's arm a squeeze before he turned to go.

"I see you two hit it off. I saw you in the hall," Raquelle said as they were both loading their coats into their lockers.

"Yes. . . . I think you could definitely say so," Katie agreed dreamily. She stifled a yawn.

As they walked into their first class of the day, Raquelle moved toward her seat in the back of the room, and Katie started to sit down in her usual spot in the second row.

Before she could sit down, the teacher, Mr. Preston, motioned Katie aside.

"I'd like to have a word with you, Ms. Shaw, about the quality of your work lately. It just hasn't been up to par. Carelessness is very unusual for you, and I'm really rather surprised. I hope you have an explanation."

Katie was crushed. She had never heard anything like this from a teacher before. All she could do was shake her head and promise to be careful.

She had an explanation all right.

She just couldn't tell him what it was.

Chapter 16

Katie didn't study after school. She went out with Jason instead.

I'll study tomorrow, Katie thought as she came home and got ready for bed. Having fun with Jason had driven the thoughts of her conference with the teacher from Katie's mind.

They had gone to Fuzzy's — a local after-school hangout. It was really great to walk in as a couple (as Jason's girlfriend) — to be somebody, and be part of the crowd.

Katie had gone there alone a few times when she had started school but she hadn't spoken to anyone, and no one spoke to her. Now things were different.

Now Katie was . . . *popular.* She didn't even have to work at being the center of attention — it just happened.

I've changed so much, she thought.

Heath told me he'd make it all possible.

Did he?

As Katie got into bed she took out her diary. Propping herself against the pillows, she began to write.

Dear Diary,

I know I haven't written in a while, but so much has happened so fast. I'm hardly like the old Katie at all. Sometimes I'm not even sure who I am, or if I deserve such a wonderful life.

Did all this happen because of Heath Granger? Do I have Heath to thank for Raquelle, and all my other friends? Did Heath give me the nerve enough to change? Is Heath even real?

Katie put her pen down and stared out at the moon. She started to think about Jason, remembering his poem — a sweet, funny "love letter."

That's it. Love letter. I'll get Heath to write me a love letter, and when I wake up I'll have it — to prove he's real.

To prove that I didn't just imagine him.

Katie didn't *really* want a love letter from Heath. Not anymore.

If Heath knows I went out with Jason after school he might not want to write me a love letter anyway. Who knows what he might do?

The thought made Katie twist the sheet in her hands.

Katie wished she could predict what Heath would find out. Sometimes he knew everything that happened in her life as if he'd seen it on a movie screen. Other times she was surprised at what he didn't catch.

There seemed to be no pattern to it, but she'd keep trying to find out. Of course, she'd thought of the possibility that Heath wasn't telling her everything he knew.

Chapter 17

Katie had only been asleep for a few minutes that night when she saw Heath, leaning against the tree in front of the house as he usually did.

His smile was wide and warm as Katie walked across the yard, and there were no sullen looks or reproaches for her being late. Instead, the first thing he said to her was, "I wish you'd stay here all the time with me, Katie. Isn't it beautiful? It's never cold here. It's always sunny and warm. You'd be my girl — always. Imagine — no more homework, no more scolding teachers. What could be so bad about living endlessly in a beautiful dream."

No way! Katie thought. *Why did this have to happen to me?*

Wait a minute. Katie went over everything Heath had just said, and her heart felt cold.

How does he know about the teacher scolding me?

"How did you know about the scolding teacher?" she asked.

"Well, you were thinking about him before you went to sleep, weren't you? It was a very strong thought. I just — pick up things sometimes. Never can tell what."

Heath's smile made her think he was hiding something.

Did he know she thought about Jason, too?

Katie saw that Heath was unable to keep the smug expression off his face. *He's doing this on purpose, to keep me guessing. To confuse me.*

"Could you tell that there's something I've been hoping you'd do?"

Heath looked as if he'd been thrown a curve he wasn't expecting.

Good, Katie thought.

"I've been hoping you'd write me a love letter. I've never had one."

Katie watched Heath's face. More confusion. *Hallelujah!*

"Look, I even brought a pen and some paper for you." Katie had fallen asleep clutching them in her hands. Now she gave them to Heath. He was still standing with a blank expression on his face.

Will he decide this is a job for Mr. Wonderful, Mr. McNasty, or The Poor Little Boy?

Katie crossed her fingers and hoped for Mr. Wonderful.

"Okay," Heath said, finally. "Women! It's not going to be long. I'm no poet."

"It's okay. I'm sure if you care for me the way you say you do, you'll find the perfect thing to say."

As Heath trudged away, he remembered to turn around and flash Katie a dazzling smile. He sat on the edge of the porch writing, while Katie sat on the steps waiting.

In a few moments he returned, tapped her on the shoulder, and handed her the paper, folded in half.

Katie opened it, and it read:

I LOVE YOU
KATIE BLUE

"It's about your blue eyes."

"Oh, thank you." Katie squeezed his hand.

I guess English wasn't your favorite subject, Heath. Well, at least it's something.

Katie clutched the five words in her hand.

"Now give it back." Heath held out his hand for the note.

Katie hadn't counted on this.

"You don't give *back* love letters, Heath."

"Give it back."

Katie knew she wasn't going to be able to reason him out of it, coax him out of it, or tease him out of it.

She clutched the note firmly in her hand and concentrated as hard as she could. *WAKE UP!*

Chapter 18

It worked. I'm awake and I'm still holding his letter in my hand.

Katie sat up in bed and rubbed her eyes.

What is that smell?

An acrid, burning heat filled her lungs. A thick curtain of smoke hung in the air. Katie jumped out of bed. Her hands flew to the sides of her face in surprise as she saw where the smoke was coming from.

There were sparks and little flames coming from the lamp cord on her bedside table. The flames danced brightly toward each other as if trying to ignite a larger flame.

Katie stood transfixed as the lace doily underneath the lamp started to burn. She didn't realize that she'd dropped the precious note from Heath, and that it had fallen on the table until the flames started licking at its edges. It was reduced to ashes before she could even think of saving it.

Katie pushed all thoughts of the letter to the back of her mind as she concentrated on putting out the fire. She grabbed a pillow from the bed and, coughing from the smoke, started to beat the blaze.

The flames fought for their lives but were soon smothered. As Katie battered the blaze, the lamp was knocked over. As it fell the weight pulled the plug from the wall. Sparks shot out of the socket like fireworks, but soon died leaving black, sooty stains.

Then it was over. Katie threw down the pillow. Flames had eaten away part of it, leaving a gaping circle of charred feathers surrounded by singed cloth.

Katie threw open a window and took in great gulps of air. She wondered for the millionth time why her parents hadn't had this old house rewired before they moved in. It was really dangerous.

Katie walked back to the table and stared at the ashen remains of what was to have been her proof of Heath's existence. It was just a pile of ashes, indistinguishable from the rest.

She crumbled the ashes between her fingers

regretfully, and then swept the whole mess into the wastebasket.

All for nothing. Katie wanted to cry.

That won't do any good, she told herself. *You've just got to find another way to prove he's real.*

For the moment, though, Katie had no energy to think of another plan. She only felt drained and discouraged.

She slumped into an overstuffed chair in the corner of her room and stared out the window, not really seeing anything.

The movement of what seemed like a shadow caused her to turn away from the window.

It wasn't a shadow.

Katie scrambled to her feet and covered her mouth with her hand. She drew in her breath sharply.

Heath had always waited for her outside under the tree in the front yard.

Now he was in her room, sitting in the chair at her dressing table, staring at her with the most awful look in his eyes.

"You tricked me into writing a letter so you could bring it back here, didn't you?" Heath had the look of a menacing cobra, poised and ready to strike.

"Yes," Katie said in a small voice.

Heath rose to his feet and was across the room in two strides.

"I don't want you playing tricks on me — trying to take things out of the dream ever again. *EVER, EVER!* Do you understand?"

Katie nodded in silence.

"You put the ashes in here?" Heath barked, indicating the wastebasket.

Katie nodded again, and looked away. Her gaze fell on the overstuffed easy chair.

What she saw made her insides lurch.

Katie had looked down at her own sleeping body. It was such an eerie feeling, like those movies where the soul looks down on the dead body that formerly housed it. She felt nauseous.

This time it's not a movie. This time I'm looking at myself.

But you're not dead — you're only dreaming, she reminded herself.

Katie looked back at Heath, whose face wore a contemptuous smirk. "Squeamish, are we? Too bad." He shrugged. "Well, I guess I'm finished here now."

He shook his finger in Katie's face. "Remember, everything from the dream stays in the dream."

Then he was gone.

Then he was back.

"Do you have a diary?" he snapped.

"Yes. Yes."

"Then tell me where it is!" The words had the force of a slap.

"It's in the drawer — in the table by the bed." Katie heard her words come out in a tight unfamiliar squeak.

Heath pulled the drawer out, throwing the contents on the floor. He picked the diary out of the pile of things strewn on the rug, and held it to his chest for a moment, eyes closed. Then he threw it in the corner of the room.

Now he fixed his eyes on Katie with a glowering stare. "Don't write about me again. Don't write about me, and don't talk about me!"

And then he vanished.

The clock radio blared, and the alarm clock was clanging away when Kate awoke. For a moment she stared uncomprehendingly at the black stains slashed on the wall, the charred lamp cord and cloud of soot and ash around the lamp. Then she hugged her knees for a moment, trembling, as everything came back to her.

Katie's diary was lying on the floor, in the corner of the room near the window. She got out of bed and picked it up. Then she reached under the mattress, where she kept the key, tied on a long ribbon.

Hands shaking, she unlocked the diary. She thumbed through it. At first, everything seemed to be just as it was.

But when she got to the part of the diary where she'd started writing about Heath, the writing was unreadable. The pages were covered thickly with the wild scribbles of an unseen hand.

Chapter 19

"Something wrong?"

"No, Raquelle, there's nothing wrong." Katie had a hard time concealing her impatience. She often felt edgy these days. "I guess I'm just tired. I haven't been sleeping very well lately. It'll pass."

"Okay." Raquelle shrugged.

If only I could talk to her. If only I could talk to somebody, Katie wished as she sat in Mr. Preston's English class.

Katie tried to pay attention and not slump but she was so tired. Every once in a while, Mr. Preston would shoot a disapproving look her way.

Mind your own business, Katie wanted to snap. She felt like he was hoping to catch her in one wrong move.

I've got to pay attention, Katie told herself again and again.

She propped her chin in her hands.

She gripped her pen tightly.

There was a close call as Katie realized that her eyelids were drooping just in time to open wide as Mr. Preston turned to face the class.

Can't catch me, Katie thought smugly.

But soon she couldn't hold on any longer. The room started to swirl around her, and Katie was riding on a carousel she couldn't get off. Then she was falling, falling through a dark, bottomless pit.

It seemed that she fell forever before she landed, her back against something solid and hard. She was on her back, staring up at the sky. All the wind had been knocked out of her.

"Having trouble concentrating?" Heath's face suddenly loomed above her. Katie looked up at him as she realized she was lying on the porch steps.

I'm back at home . . . but I can't be. That means I'm in my class, ASLEEP!

Katie scrambled to her feet. "What are you doing?" she yelled at Heath. "I'm supposed to be in my English class, paying attention to a lecture. Do you realize how it looks? The teacher will find me there, asleep at my desk!"

Heath threw back his head and laughed. "That's not my problem, Katie. You're just taking a little break to pay attention to me, instead."

What if someone in class hears him, Katie worried. She pressed a finger to her lips. "Shhhhh."

"Shhhh!" Heath mimicked nastily. He raked his fingers through his hair.

"Don't worry, Miss Goody Two Shoes. They can't hear us. Unless you start snoring, that is."

"Why are you doing this, Heath? Why?"

Heath sneered. "Because I *can.*"

He walked a few paces. "I felt lively, and I didn't feel like waiting for you. Now is as good a time as any to let you know that things have changed. I'm through playing along with you, now you're going to play along with *me.*"

He thinks he's been playing along with me? Katie whispered to herself incredulously.

"From now on, Katie, you're going to meet me exactly when I tell you to. I'm through waiting for you to dream me up. From now on *I* decide."

He stared at Katie for a moment, relishing her confusion. "You just don't get it, do you? Well, get this. At first I had to let you run the show — decide when you'd go to sleep, when you wanted to be with me, and when you wanted to be elsewhere."

Heath paced back and forth in front of Katie as he spoke. "But the more you napped, or went to bed early, or overslept, the more time you spent dreaming me, the stronger I became."

Katie gripped the porch rail. Of course. That's why he always wanted her to be with him more, and more, and more. That's why she was always tired, and had starting dozing off. Heath was taking something from her — some sort of energy.

She didn't want to believe it . . . though in her heart she knew it was true. "You're bluffing, Heath. You're just trying to scare me."

Heath smiled. *Like the spider to the fly*, Katie thought.

"Think I'm bluffing? Well, I never got you out of class before, did I? Don't fight me Katie, you can't win."

Heath gestured at the surrounding countryside. "Isn't this better than being in school? Come on Katie, I'm a real charming guy. Better than that sandy-eyed mama's boy, Jason."

Katie felt as if the breath had been slammed out of her at the mention of Jason's name.

Heath knew.

He walked toward Katie.

She backed up.

"You might say I'm a dream come true for

you, Katie," Heath smiled cryptically. "You might as well get to like it, and you'd better stay on my good side because you know what? One of these days I could be the one dreaming *you* up!"

Heath's laughter echoed in Katie's ears.

Then she fainted.

"Wake up, Katie, wake up!" The voice got louder and louder. Someone was shaking her, hard.

"Stop it! Stop it!" Katie opened her eyes and shook her head back and forth.

She was back in the classroom.

I fell asleep in class, she realized. *I fell asleep in class.*

Chapter 20

"Have you been taking drugs, Katie?" Mr. Preston asked, in front of the whole class. "Have you been drinking?" He leaned close to her and inhaled, obviously.

Katie thought that the sight of Mr. Preston's face so close to hers was terrible to behold. She could see the enlarged, crater-like pores on his chin. She could see the hair in his nose. Katie raised her head from the desk.

Mr. Preston insisted that she accompany him to the office of Suzanne Fusco, the guidance counselor. Katie agreed to go along only on the condition that he didn't call her parents. He had agreed, at least for the present.

"We'll see what Ms. Fusco thinks," he told Katie.

Inside her office, Ms. Fusco smiled at Katie. *The kind of smile salespeople give you when they hand you your change and say "Have a nice day,"* Katie thought. It made Katie want to wring her hands in despair.

"I'm not taking drugs and I haven't been drinking," Katie said, feeling terribly embarrassed. She looked down into her lap. *Drugs indeed! I won't even take a sleeping pill.*

"Be careful to tell us the truth, Katie," Mr. Preston said.

Tell you the truth. Ha! You'd put me in a padded room.

Katie ran her tongue over her lips. Her mouth felt dry.

"Can I have a drink of water?" She watched as Ms. Fusco and Mr. Preston exchanged glances.

"Why are you looking at each other like that? I asked for a drink of water. Is that supposed to mean I'm a drug addict?"

After an uncomfortable silence, Mr. Preston excused himself.

"I haven't formed any opinions yet, Katie. Mr. Preston isn't the only one of your teachers to express concern about the change in your behavior. Why don't you just tell me what you think is going on." Ms. Fusco settled back in her chair.

"What do you mean 'going on'?" Katie said, sullenly.

Suzanne Fusco sat up and faced Katie squarely.

"I'm not going to play games with you, Katie. The drop in your grades is serious."

"I don't want you to say anything to my parents."

Ms. Fusco was silent for a moment.

"Okay, Katie. We'll do it your way — for a while. But you'd better be straight with me. If you don't seem to be doing anything to harm yourself, we'll leave it all right here. That's the best I can promise you."

Katie took a deep breath. *How much to tell? How much to hold back?* "I've been having nightmares — trouble sleeping," she said finally. "I guess that's why I was so tired, I fell asleep in class."

"When did all this start?"

"Shortly after I moved here." Katie twisted her hands. She didn't like to lie, but why mention that she'd had trouble sleeping before she moved here, too?

"I've been looking at your file, Katie," Ms. Fusco said, indicating a folder on her desk.

What's in there? Katie wondered.

"It looks like you were basically a studious sort, before you came here. Now you're a regular social butterfly." She smiled.

Katie nodded, trying to keep her eyelids from drooping.

"By the way, your outfit is very fashionable."

"Thanks," Katie said. *What's she up to now?*

"You know," the counselor droned on, "sometimes when we try too hard to be something we're not — it backfires and causes us other problems. Why not just try to be yourself?"

Katie wanted to scream and throw up her hands. *Be careful,* she told herself.

"I'll keep that in mind," she said evenly.

Ms. Fusco looked a little disconcerted. This obviously wasn't the reaction she expected.

What does she want? Katie wondered. She searched for the right words, the way a mouse seeks its way out of a maze.

"I think I've gotten some insight out of this talk with you, Ms. Fusco. It's really been helpful. Can I go now? I'm really tired." She picked up her books.

Ms. Fusco still looked disappointed, though a little less so than before. She nodded, and Katie left the office.

The hallway was deserted. The last class of the day had already started. The students sat in classrooms behind closed doors.

As Katie heard her footsteps echoing in the

hall, she felt isolated in a way she never had before.

She supposed Ms. Fusco was only trying to help. Katie wished she could've talked to her. She really did. Telling the story of what had happened with Heath would have brought such relief.

It was horrible to be locked inside alone with him.

However, Ms. Fusco didn't strike Katie as the type of person who would have given the story any credence. *It's hard to imagine anyone who would,* Katie smiled grimly.

No, Ms. Fusco would immediately have me fitted for a straitjacket.

Chapter 21

Katie didn't bother going to her last class. She didn't want to face anyone who had seen her fall asleep in class or who had heard Mr. Preston ask her if she'd been taking drugs or been drinking.

It was so humiliating. *Better to just go home*, she thought.

Later, alone in her room, she sat at her dressing table staring blankly into the mirror. In it she saw the face of a girl who was thinner than Katie remembered — who stared back at her with wide, frightened eyes full of feverish brilliance.

It was as if she was staring at the face of someone she thought she ought to know — but wasn't sure she remembered.

Suddenly the room grew hotter. *Hotter, hotter, hotter*. Perspiration rolled in huge droplets from Katie's forehead. She was just about to get up and open the window, when the reflection in the mirror changed.

The droplets that trickled down her face were no longer perspiration. They were like candle drippings. Katie's face was . . . melting. Flesh rolled from her skull like huge blobs of hot wax, landing on the dressing table.

Plop.

Plop.

As Katie watched in a trance, the flesh continued to flow until an entire side of her skull was exposed. The horrified eye stared out of a boney socket.

Plop.

Plop.

It wasn't long before Katie's skull stared back at her from the mirror. The teeth seemed to grin at her.

Katie was so terrified that her hair was standing away from her face.

The hideous vision of the fleshless skull in a fright wig would have been horrible to behold, even in a movie. But it inspired unknown terrors as Katie realized it was a reflection of herself.

And then, *horribly*, Katie watched as masses of cockroaches poured from the grinning, lipless skull.

Then she heard the laughter. Heath's reflection was in the mirror. He was standing behind her.

"Do you like this game? It's called *Illusion.*"

The reflection of the revolting, cockroach-infested skull vanished suddenly, and Katie's own frightened face stared back at her from the glass.

Katie whirled around to face Heath. She was sick with revulsion.

"Want to play another one?"

Katie shook her head with the little energy she had left. "No . . . " she breathed.

Was it possible that I thought Heath couldn't do anything worse? That Heath had shown all the terrors he had to offer? Not so.

"Don't be a party pooper. Do you get the message, Katie? *Don't make me mad.*"

As Katie ran toward the bathroom, she could hear Heath's laughter echoing in her ears. Hanging on to the sink, she bent over the toilet bowl and threw up until she was too dizzy to stand. Then the blackness started closing in all around the edges of her vision . . . and then there was only emptiness.

Katie didn't know how long she remained on the bathroom floor. When she woke up, the smell of sickness hung in the air, and the house was quiet.

She pulled herself into a sitting position,

back up against the shower stall. She looked at the clock on the counter beside the sink.

Impossible.

She had been at home for only *ten minutes*!

After sitting on the floor for an hour, Katie got up and brushed her teeth. Twice. Followed by an extra long mouthwash rinse.

Then she walked back into her room.

The vision was so real. What did Heath call his game?

Illusion.

Katie hoped they wouldn't be playing it again, but she knew they probably would.

One thing was for certain.

Heath was getting stronger.

And that was not all.

He was getting *meaner*.

Chapter 22

A wave of dark exhaustion washed over Katie, commanding her to sleep again after only a few blessed moments of wakeful relief. She was swept into the dream once more — so swiftly that the sharp taste of toothpaste and mouthwash still lingered on her lips.

"Did you enjoy my little game?" Heath was grinning from ear to ear. "Incredible, wasn't it?"

That I ever had the illusion that you were charming is what's incredible, Katie thought, as she listened to him gloating over the terror he had caused her. *About as charming as a carrion vulture.*

"And you thought I was just a figment of your imagination. Well, whoa girl! It looks like your imagination has run wild!" Heath laughed.

Death-rattle cackle, Katie thought.

"We don't have to play *Illusion* anymore, if you start keeping up your end of the bargain.

You promised to be *my special girl.* Isn't that what we agreed when we started . . . meeting like this?" Heath looked at her pointedly.

My special girl. Katie cringed. *What a revolting idea.*

What's he up to? she wondered.

"I said I'd help you find yourself, and I did. Just look at how you've changed, how you look — all the friends you have."

Oh, please, Heath, even my parents never gave me the famous after-all-I've-done-for-you speech.

"Without me, Katie, you'd be nothing. Nothing more than the plain, quiet, timid girl you were before."

Is that true, Heath? Or have you made it up to intimidate me all along. I've asked myself that question over and over, and the answer seems to be NO. You don't seem to be the kind of person who'd want to help me — or to help anybody.

You said you'd help me, and I fell for the power of suggestion, but I'm the one who took it from there.

No, Heath. The truth is that without me you'd *be nothing. I just can't figure out how to get rid of you.*

"How did you repay me? By going out with another guy. Than you tried to trick me with that love letter business of yours."

The sight of Heath strutting around as he spoke self-righteously about honesty was almost too much for Katie. In spite of her fear, it was an effort to keep from laughing.

Heath was warming up to his role as the wronged victim.

"You deliberately do something without checking with me to see if I might get hurt. I had to go back and get that letter."

Heath's face twisted. "You have no idea of the pain it —"

Heath looked aware that he'd let something slip. He broke off suddenly, knitted his brows together, and ran a hand over his mouth.

Katie pounced on his last sentence eagerly. "Tell me what kind of things could hurt you and I'll be careful not to do them."

I'll be careful not to do them one at a time. I'll do them all together. Hope you enjoy it. Hope it blasts you out of my life.

Heath spat into the dirt. "Yes, wouldn't that be nice, if I'd make sure to let you know about anything that could hurt me. You'd be real careful."

Heath shoved his hands deep into his pockets. "You'd better start keeping up your end of the bargain. And quit playing tricks. Or something unpleasant might happen."

Might happen? Katie wanted to shout. *Might happen? Haven't plenty of unpleasant things already happened?*

"You wouldn't want to wake up one morning and find out you'd been walking in your sleep and done something . . . terrible. Maybe gone down to the kitchen and gotten a knife out of the drawer . . . a big knife? Maybe gone after that dog, or gone back upstairs and into your parents' room?"

The horror of what he'd just suggested brought Katie up short so fast that she even forgot to breathe for a moment. Then she gasped.

What kind of psychopathic monster talked about killing your whole family in the same tone they'd use to say, "Please pass the peas"?

"You just watch yourself, Katie. I don't like being jerked around," Heath said as a parting shot.

Then he was gone.

Chapter 23

The moment Katie woke up, she reached under her pillow and pulled out the tape recorder. She had set it to record just before she fell asleep.

With trembling hands she rewound the tape and pushed the play button. The cassette reels started to turn.

Come on, come on, Katie prayed.

And then she heard it. The sound was garbled and faint, but Katie could make out the words.

"YOU'D BETTER START KEEPING UP YOUR END OF THE BARGAIN. AND QUIT PLAYING TRICKS. OR SOMETHING UNPLEASANT MIGHT HAPPEN. . . . I DON'T LIKE BEING JERKED AROUND."

The sound of Heath's voice sent a hot, prickly sensation up Katie's spine.

Well, at last I got him, she thought, switching off the tape.

She sighed and sank back into the pillows, feeling drained.

She pushed the rewind and then the play button again. *I guess I've just got to be sure I heard what I thought I heard.*

She laughed aloud.

I've got to make sure I'm not dreaming.

Sure enough, it was Heath's voice on the tape sounding sneering, threatening.

Katie switched off the machine.

If it's really harmful to him to have any kind of evidence brought back to this world, I wonder what's happening to him now, she wondered.

I hope it's horrible. She smiled secretly to herself.

Suddenly the tape recorder was moving in Katie's hand. The reels were turning . . . backwards. The erase button was depressed . . . and nothing Katie could do would raise it. Frantically, she pushed the off button.

A white hot flash of pain blazed through her head without warning. It was as if someone had driven a burning spike into her brain. She was paralyzed.

The sensation made her eyes glaze over. As she sat on the bed, motionless, the walls of the room began to move in a violent, waving motion. The glass in the windows began to rattle. A chair overturned with a crash, and books flew off the shelves.

Gripping the tape recorder tightly, Katie jumped out of bed and started to run for the door, but a hot gust of air rushed over her with such force that she was held in one spot. The force of the air grew stronger until it blew her off her feet.

A series of unearthly wails and howls issued from the tape recorder.

BUT I TURNED IT OFF! Now Katie tried to let go of the tape recorder, but it refused to leave her hands. Horrified, she held the machine at arm's length as the howls were replaced by a voice — Heath's voice. But the words weren't what Katie had recorded. Heath was talking to her.

"You want to hear my voice? Is that why you did what you did? Have you any idea of the pain you've caused me by taking my voice and putting it on this thing? The pain is worse than THIS!"

Again the burning flash cut into Katie's skull. This time it sent her sprawling on the floor.

"I'll make sure you hear my voice a lot, now," Heath continued. The sound of his voice was a terrifying combination of rage and madness.

"I'm going to echo inside your brain until you wish you were dead."

The tape recorder she was holding began growing hotter and hotter.

Katie shook her hands frantically, trying to break free of the machine that was burning her. But it was stuck to her hands as if it were glued.

The pain brought tears to her eyes. Katie held on helplessly as hot pain seeped into the bones of her hand and up her arm.

The machine was "eating" the tape, turning it into a twisted tangled mass. Finally, when there was nothing left of it, the recorder fell from Katie's hands.

A thin stream of smoke poured from the tape recorder as it gave up the ghost, and died.

The pain was subsiding. Katie was sure that when she looked at her hands she'd see nothing but charred stumps.

When she could stand the fear no longer, she held her hands in front of her eyes.

It was as if nothing had happened. Her hands weren't charred. There weren't even any blisters.

Chapter 24

Heath's tape recorder visitation marked the beginning of Katie's campaign of not sleeping.

Of course I'll have to sleep some time, she reasoned. *But I'll deal with that when the time comes.*

The first night she slogged through a term paper for Mr. Preston's English class. It was an analysis of several short stories. Katie thought it was turning out to be as good as any of the work she'd done before — maybe better. Mr. Preston wouldn't have anything to complain about.

Staying awake all night is easy, Katie thought as she watched the sun rise. *After all, I've done it before, though never on purpose.*

As she got ready for school, she remembered the eyedrops she'd bought at the drugstore.

She'd never used eyedrops before, and at first she felt a little squeamish as she tilted her head back and squeezed the bottle. She blinked several times, but at last got the drops in her eyes.

"Well, that wasn't so bad after all," she said to her reflection in the mirror as she blotted around her eyes with a tissue. *That ought to take care of the redness, now let's do something about the dark circles.*

Katie had already been using a cover-up on the circles under her eyes. She wanted to stave off comments like, "You look *exhausted.*" After patting the makeup under her eyes she congratulated herself on a job well done. "You look great, not one person will ever know."

True, she felt a little tired, but she hoped coffee would take care of that. Katie decided to drive to school. It was still early and she'd have time to stop at Trixie's Diner and have breakfast — with several cups of coffee.

Katie's secret hope was that if she didn't go to sleep for a while, it would take away some of Heath's strength. Maybe she could even make him fade away all together.

She didn't really believe that part, but it was nice to think about.

Why didn't he try to make me fall asleep last night? The thought flashed in Katie's mind like a red warning light. He'd pulled her into sleep plenty of times before. *What happened?*

She was glad he didn't do it last night, but it worried her, too. Whenever Heath did something unusual, she wondered if he was planning some new trick — a new terror for her.

When the day sped by without any disasters, Katie thought she was on to a good idea. She decided to try another sleepless night.

This time it wasn't so easy.

After she finished her homework, she turned on the TV. A few hours of watching, and she was bored. Besides, there was nothing left to watch at that late hour that was any good. *Why can't we get cable out here?* she grumbled inwardly as she threw the TV listings on the floor.

The night was certainly dragging by. It reminded Katie of her nights of insomnia, when she'd tossed and turned and prayed for sleep.

How strange — she thought she could fall asleep in a second, but now she was trying *not to*.

Heath didn't seem to be around. Katie didn't feel him exerting any pull, any force at all. She could tell the difference in the way she felt — this was normal sleepiness.

She felt another yawn coming on. "I'm so sick of yawning!" Katie gave a pile of books on her dresser a shove that sent them crashing to the floor. *Want to wake everybody up?* she scolded herself.

For a moment Katie thought of giving up the whole idea and going to sleep.

Then she remembered what Heath said about sleepwalking. She didn't think he could make her hurt her parents — or Bopper — but she couldn't be sure.

In the mirror over her dresser, Katie could see a pimple beginning to emerge on her chin. She dabbed cold water on her face from a pitcher full of ice cubes she'd brought upstairs.

Then she put on headphones and turned on her Walkman with the music playing full blast. She flipped through fashion magazines. It was too hard to concentrate on reading a book.

After a while Katie went downstairs and made a pot of coffee. It was a good thing the directions were on the package, because she'd never made it before.

Still, she put in a lot more coffee than the directions called for. She wanted to make sure it was good and strong.

After the coffee brewed, she poured herself a big cup. She decided to drink it black. Maybe it would be more potent that way.

Phew! Katie thought, downing a mouthful with difficulty. It was strong, all right. But not very good.

After Katie finished her second cup of coffee,

she noticed that her hands were shaking.

It was daylight, now, and Katie knew there was no way she'd be able to drive to work in her present condition. Just the thought conjured up all sorts of terrifying visions — the sight of herself asleep at the wheel, running the car into a ditch, or getting into an accident and killing someone.

Pictures of auto accidents she'd seen on the news came to mind. *The ambulances. The blood.*

Katie shuddered.

I don't want to wait for the bus. Who knows what Biff would say if he caught me taking a little snooze again. If one of the Tippler twins so much as crossed her little beady eyes at me, I'd tear her hair out.

She didn't want to stick around and make small talk with her parents over breakfast, either.

Katie decided to walk.

She poured the remaining contents of the coffeepot into a thermos, and then cleaned the pot carefully. Her parents were sure to think something was up if they knew she'd made a pot of coffee, and the last thing she wanted to do was to arouse their suspicions any further.

Katie did her best, but the eyedrops and

concealer didn't work the same magic this morning. The pimple on her chin now glowed an angry red.

The fuchsia dress she put on, and her Mexican silver earrings, couldn't compensate for the sallowness of her skin, either.

Katie put on extra blusher and told herself she looked fine. But she felt strange — off balance, not herself.

All the way to school, Katie had the feeling she was being followed. She turned around quickly several times, sure that she'd heard a noise — seen a shadow.

But each time she did, no one was there.

Chapter 25

"Nice dress, Katie. But gee, you look — wasted. Should you be in school? Are you sick or something?" Raquelle's brown eyes were wide.

"Why don't you try minding your own business once in a while, Raquelle? I mean, Rachel." Katie slammed her locker shut and stomped into class, leaving Raquelle standing there, openmouthed.

Why does she have to compliment everything I wear? For the first time, Katie wondered if Raquelle was jealous.

When Raquelle walked by Katie's desk on her way to her seat in the back row, Katie kept her eyes fixed on a paper in front of her. She didn't look at Raquelle.

She might as well know I can see right through her, Katie said to herself, trying to feel right about what she'd just done. But the uncomfortable feeling wouldn't let go of her, especially after a girl in the next row asked her if she felt okay.

Katie was glad Jason wasn't at school that day. She was sorry he was home sick, but she didn't want him to see her looking the way she did.

Katie concentrated on keeping her glassy-eyed gaze fixed on Mr. Preston's face. At least he had commended her on producing some fine work at the end of class.

"That was a terrific job on the paper, Katie. That's the kind of work I'm used to seeing from you. Glad to see you're back on track."

Katie nodded stiffly and she mumbled, "Thanks."

"Oh, but Katie," Mr. Preston called as she turned to leave.

What now? she wondered irritably. She forced herself to turn around and look at Mr. Preston with what she hoped was a polite expression.

"You look a little peaked, Katie. I want good work but there's no need to push yourself *too* hard. I don't want you to make yourself sick."

Katie turned and left without a word. "Why can't everybody make up their minds about what they want from me," she muttered under her breath.

Actually, Katie didn't feel very well. But when she thought of going home, she became fearful of going to sleep. *At least at school I have a better chance of staying awake*, she told herself.

Before her last class she stopped at her locker and got out the thermos. She downed a quick cup of coffee, trying to ignore the curious gazes of passing students. She wanted to shout something rude at them.

Katie saw that her hands were shaking again. She was unable to control it, and could only watch helplessly as the thermos and cup slipped from her grasp and crashed to the floor. Hot coffee cascaded all over the hallway. Some of the steaming liquid splashed on Katie, burning her legs and staining the hem of her dress.

Katie kicked at the thermos. Passersby gawked at her as they tried to maneuver around the coffee pools.

"What are you looking at? Didn't you ever drop anything?" Katie said angrily. People looked at each other and raised their eyebrows as they walked by.

Then someone was there, helping Katie pick up the thermos. Pulling a wastebasket out of a classroom and throwing part of it away.

It was Raquelle.

"I'm sorry about what I said to you before.

I'm really *not* feeling well," Katie said apologetically.

"That's okay." Raquelle put her hand on Katie's shoulder. "I knew something had to be the matter. Look, don't touch anything. The liner of the thermos broke and there's glass all over. I'll get a janitor to help us. Why don't you go get tidied up?"

"Thanks," Katie said.

"Hey, Katie," Raquelle smiled as she turned away, "you talk to me like that again, and you've had it."

Katie smiled back and shook her head. Then she walked to the restroom.

She ran cold water in the sink and splashed it on her face.

I wish I could tell Raquelle what is really the matter, but what would I say? "Hey, Raquelle, there's this guy in my dream who's trying to ruin my life, and I'm so afraid of him, I'm scared to go to sleep."

Katie dabbed at the coffee stains on the hem of her skirt. Suddenly she jumped. She thought she saw a bug crawling on her leg. But when she went to hit it away, it wasn't there.

That's when she noticed the cobwebs hanging from her hands. She tried to brush them away, but more appeared. She rubbed her hands again and again, but the cobwebs remained.

What on earth is happening to me?

She looked in the mirror as if searching for an answer. There were little white soap spots on the edge of the mirror, she noticed.

Soap spots?

How could soap spots be moving?

Then the soap spots started turning into something else.

Katie watched in horror as a group of white worms crawled across the reflection of her face.

Chapter 26

Katie ran from the restroom and flew to her locker. Raquelle hadn't returned with the janitor yet. The mess from the broken thermos was still lying on the hall floor.

Grabbing her coat, Katie ran from the building. She didn't stop running until she reached her house.

Little flames leaped out of the keyhole when she opened the front door. *Heath is back,* she said to herself.

There was no way she could delay sleep for more than a few minutes, however. It took a huge effort not to fall asleep on the stairs.

Katie forced herself to keep moving until she reached her room. She was barely able to hang up her clothes and change into her nightgown before she fell on the pillows and into sleep.

Heath was waiting for her. "Well, gee, I was beginning to think we weren't pals anymore."

His smile was smug and his eyes gleamed with that snakelike quality Katie had seen before. "Come around more often. Don't make yourself a stranger."

Heath shook his head as if to say *shame on you*. "Sometimes it scares me, how perceptive I am," he said. "How can I be such a clever guy? I knew you'd try to pull something like staying awake sooner or later. That's not very smart. A girl needs her beauty sleep."

As Katie watched him, she was suddenly aware that the feeling of exhaustion had left her entirely. *Great*, she thought. *All day long I stumble around in a daze, and the only time I feel wide-awake is when I'm asleep.*

Heath tossed his hair off his forehead. It was a gesture Katie would have found irresistable not too long ago. She turned away from him. Was it possible he was as good-looking as before? She really couldn't tell — she found everything about him so unappealing.

"Why are you tormenting me?" Katie turned back to him. "If you hate me so much, why don't you go and haunt someone else?"

Heath opened his mouth to say something, but apparently thought better of it. He was silent for a few moments before he spoke.

"I'm not going to give you another warning. The more you try playing these games with me, the worse it's going to get."

Heath was pacing back and forth now, moving like a caged panther. "As for staying awake to try and get rid of me, forget it. It's too bad you didn't read up on your subject a little bit. In this case, the subject is dreams."

Heath tapped his head with his finger. "I've always loved to read, that's why I've always got the edge." He pointed his finger at her. "Katie, let me tell you what I read about dreams. Nobody can do without them. If you stay awake so you don't dream, do you know what happens? You just make up for it by dreaming more than ever when you finally go to sleep."

Heath looked pleased with himself. He slouched back against the tree and cocked his head to one side. "Since you haven't had any sleep for the past couple nights, you're going to be doing a whole lot of dreaming."

Katie's heart sank to her knees. Was he telling the truth? If he was, then the torture she'd put herself through had all been for nothing.

Heath did a lazy shrug. "Might as well make yourself at home. We're going to be spending quite a bit of time together."

Chapter 27

Katie stirred, gazing at the Saturday morning sunlight filtering through the curtains on her bedroom window. She threw an arm across her face, shielding her eyes.

I'm awake.

For a few blissful moments Katie relished a kind of temporary amnesia in which there were no bad dreams and no terrifying visions. She was just a girl enjoying a sudden social success, with new friends, a wardrobe of new clothes, a variety of interests which held the promise of a bright future, and the prospect of a date this evening with a wonderful guy.

Too quickly the recollection of recent events came rushing in on her.

But at least I don't feel tired. Katie was thankful for that.

Hours of sleep had given her a renewed sense of well-being.

She heard the clock on her bedside table ticking relentlessly on. Eleven o'clock! Katie gave the timepiece a dirty look as she pulled herself out of bed.

Why hasn't someone been banging on the door to wake me? she wondered. As she crept downstairs she tried to gear up for the watchful, questioning glances that her parents had greeted her with lately.

She'd told them that she was simply swamped with homework — making a big push with her studies because she'd just entered a new school. She hoped that explained her unusual hours, early departures and late nights. She thought they'd bought it but perhaps not entirely.

But no one with suspicious eyes greeted her. The house was quiet. In the kitchen she found a note tacked on the refrigerator door with a candy-cane magnet.

She read it quickly.

"Of course!" Katie smiled to herself. She had forgotten that her parents were leaving for their vacation. They'd had to depart unusually early; that's why they hadn't wakened her.

She sighed with relief and got a bowl of cereal.

What to do today? Turn myself in at the local funny farm?

But I don't think I'm crazy.

They never do.

Katie hated to think of herself as being like those people she'd seen in the movies about the insane — obsessive people — the ones who were sure they'd been sent on a special mission . . . the only ones able to save the world, people who saw things, and heard voices. Stephen King's novels were full of them.

The light's on, but nobody's home.

Got a screw loose.

The elevator doesn't go all the way up.

She remembered something Heath had said last night. "It's too bad you didn't read up on your subject. In this case, the subject is dreams."

So I'll read up on the subject. She told herself it was worth a try. Maybe there was an explanation for these strange events after all.

In truth, Katie didn't feel much hope of finding a plausible explanation for what had been happening to her, but she was clutching at straws and held on fiercely to this one.

In less than an hour she was sitting at a table at the local library. In front of her were stacked every book on sleep and dreaming she'd been able to carry over from the shelves.

She began to read.

It soon became apparent that Heath knew

what he was talking about, all right. People needed to dream, she read, and if deprived of dreaming for a period of time, there followed a phase where they dreamed more than usual to make up.

What Heath said about that was true.

Katie sighed. *I needn't have put myself through the past few days.* There seemed to be no way to withhold dreams from Heath. If she managed to go without them for a day or so, there would simply be more later.

It was another hour before Katie discovered anything more comforting.

SLEEPWALKING DOESN'T OCCUR DURING DREAMING. WHEN YOU ARE DREAMING, YOU CAN'T MOVE YOUR ARMS AND LEGS.

That means I won't wake up and find out I've murdered my whole family in a crazed dream, like Heath suggested. It was just like him to think up a cruel lie like that, Katie thought with disgust.

But it wasn't until Katie had read quite a bit more that she came upon something that brought tears to her eyes. She reached a chapter on sleep deprivation experiments. Sleep deprivation had been conducted as part of brainwashing on prisoners of war. The POW's became confused and hysterical — willing to confess to crimes they'd never committed.

Then she read about other, controlled experiments in sleep deprivation. The subjects became angry and suspicious.

Yes, that fits, she thought, remembering how she wondered if Raquelle was jealous.

But the thing that started her crying, that made her read the passage over and over again, was the one that told her about the hallucinations. *Subjects not only acted strangely. They saw things — like cobwebs on their hands . . . and crawling bugs.*

Chapter 28

Katie tried to maintain the momentary feeling of elation she'd felt about her discovery at the library as she drove toward home, but nagging doubts kept crowding in. If prolonged lack of sleep could cause hallucinations, that still didn't explain the dreams about Heath.

That, of course, brought back the question of whether or not he was real. Katie slammed her fist on the steering wheel in frustration, causing the car to swerve alarmingly.

Watch what you're doing with the car, Katie!

"Shoot!" she muttered as she passed the Quick Stop. She had meant to run in and buy some soda and chips for snacks that night. Jason was coming over and they were going to hang out, watch TV, maybe pop a movie into the VCR.

Katie went around the block and headed

back to the Quick Stop. As she pulled into a parking space in front of the store, the horn honked in the car next to her. Startled, she looked up.

It was Raquelle.

She's going to get angry at me all over again, Katie thought, feeling sick. *She'll be mad that I left school that day when she tried to help me — without even saying a word to her.*

But Raquelle jumped out of the car wearing a huge new hat and a big smile. A multicolored, shiny scarf was tied around the neck of her oversized denim jacket. "Hi, Katie. What's up?" she asked casually.

"Hi." Katie returned the greeting awkwardly. There were a few minutes of silence. Then both of them started to speak at once, followed by embarrassed laughter, and more silence.

"Nice scarf," Katie said, finally.

"It's new."

Katie nodded, and cleared her throat. "I felt sick the other day when I dropped the thermos. That's why I didn't stick around. I just went home."

Raquelle shrugged. "I figured something like that." She picked up the edge of her scarf and started twisting the fringe.

"Raquelle, thanks for helping me. And

again — I'm sorry I flew off the handle at you. It's no excuse but sometimes I've got a pretty bad temper."

But I never used to, Katie realized suddenly. *I never used to fly off the handle, and hardly ever even raised my voice. Now I'm irritable, temperamental, and moody.*

"Let's forget the whole thing," Raquelle said, dismissing it with a wave of her hand. She shivered. "For a minute I forgot how cold it was," she said, hugging herself. "You going into the store, or what?"

Suddenly Katie realized that she was freezing, too. They both dashed inside the Quick Stop.

"What's the occasion? Are you inviting the entire football team over?" Raquelle asked, wide-eyed, as she watched Katie load a "super-duper jumbo" bag of sour cream and onion-flavored potato chips and two giant torpedos of soda pop into her mini-cart.

"It's more practical, I mean more economical, to buy the large size," Katie said with authority.

"Oh, *excuse me*. Sure," Raquelle said in an exaggerated tone. "Especially if you might, just possibly, maybe, could be, at some point in your lifetime, finish those chips before they molded over or turned into rocks."

Katie examined the bag. "It's big, all right. I guess you've got a point. Jason's got a pretty hefty appetite . . . but why don't you come over and help us out?"

"Thanks," Raquelle grinned, "but I wouldn't want to leave my buddy Maxx alone."

Maxx (with two x's) was Raquelle's new boyfriend. He wrote poetry and played the drums in his own band, called WAXX. Katie had met him only once, but she thought he and Raquelle were perfect for each other.

Both were artistic, and a little offbeat.

"So, bring Maxx along," Katie coaxed. "Come on, it'll be fun."

"Are you sure?"

"Positive."

"Okay — we'll be there," Raquelle nodded.

"Then I'd better get some more soda and another bag of chips." Katie laughed at the look of astonishment that came over Raquelle's face. "Just kidding," she added.

Later, as Katie watched Raquelle disappear into her car, she had the impulse to run to her and stop her . . . and pour out the whole story of the dreams.

Maybe I'll tell her later, when she comes over, she decided. Of course, she'd have to risk the possibility that Raquelle would think she was nuts. But it was a risk that Katie was becoming more and more willing to take.

If I don't talk to somebody about this soon, it'll be true. . . . I will go nuts.

The strain of trying to pretend that everything was normal when soap spots on mirrors turned into worms and flesh melted from her face had become almost unbearable.

Chapter 29

Jason and the others weren't due for over an hour, but Katie wanted to get things ready early so she'd have plenty of time to pick out something to wear.

She poured chips from the gigantic bag into a large ceramic bowl with pink, yellow, and red Mexican designs. The brilliance of the colors had caught her eye when she'd seen it recently at a yard sale.

She thought Raquelle would like it, too.

Katie paused for a moment, noticing how oddly out of place the wild splashes of color looked amidst the gingham tablecloth, eyelet curtains, and the soft beige and yellow colonial look of the kitchen.

The bowl fairly shouted out its presence here. *It's something I never would've chosen or even noticed a short time ago*, Katie thought. *Now it doesn't fit here — and neither do I.*

How can everything have changed so much — so fast?

How can things be so wonderful and terrible at the same time?

Is there something horribly wrong with me?

Katie suddenly remembered little Chuckie Halloran, an impish kid she used to baby-sit for back home. Chuckie had heard somewhere that a brain tumor can make someone do strange things.

For weeks afterwards he would greet visitors to his home with, "Do you have a brain tumor?" the way most kids his age would tug on a sleeve and beg to tell their latest riddle. With Chuckie it wasn't, "Why did the chicken cross the road?" It was, "Do you have a brain tumor?"

Can it be that I'm so desperate to explain these dreams that I'm practically wishing for a brain tumor? Katie giggled suddenly. The thin, tinny laughter sounded so eerie and forced in the emptiness that it startled her. It was as if it hadn't come from her own mouth.

You really don't believe you have a brain tumor, Katie. What a morbid thing to be thinking about.

A sharp, cracking sound made her jump. She had been so deep in her thoughts that the surprise yanked her back to reality with an almost physical sensation.

She crept stiffly to the window and peered outside. The sky was a cold gray evening light, and little gusts of wind blew the dead leaves around in flurries. There was a tap-tap-tapping noise as it blew the bare branches of a rosebush against the wall of the house, against the glass window of the basement.

Katie exhaled sharply and then inhaled deeply. She reminded herself how nervous she had been lately.

It's the wind, blowing things around, she told herself. *Nothing more.*

Katie glanced at the clock. Her guests should arrive in about forty-five minutes. She'd better make sure she hadn't forgotten anything. Quickly, she went down her mental checklist of items. The chips were ready to serve, soda pop in the fridge. She'd cleaned up and made everything neat.

She'd rented three videos: *Psycho* and two other Hitchcock movies. Jason loved them.

That's everything. Katie checked the last item off the list.

That's it. I'm ready to get dressed.

As Katie turned to leave the kitchen, she caught sight of her reflection in the chrome refrigerator handle. Her eyes glittered and seemed unusually wide and dark, her face almost unnaturally pale.

Ghostlike — that's how I look, she said to herself. Oddly enough, the effect was rather pleasing. She looked waiflike — elfin — with a kind of not-of-this-world beauty.

Reviewing her mental checklist of things to do had calmed Katie's nerves, the way such details always did. Those things gave her a comforting feeling of precision and order, of having done all her tasks carefully; being good and being in control of her life.

Eventually, loose ends gave her a creeping sense of anxiety. Now, having made sure all was as it should be, Katie relaxed.

Feeling rather cheerful, she picked up the bright Mexican bowl of chips and started to carry it to the den. *I wonder if I should've gotten three horror movies*, she wondered. *Especially since one is* Psycho — *having three scary ones might be overkill*, she thought, laughing at her own play on words. The maniacal music in *Psycho*, the woman's screams, and the blood washing slowly down the shower drain always formed icicles down her spine.

SNAP!

At the sound of the loud cracking noise, Katie dropped the bowl from her fingers. It shattered to pieces — a mess of brilliant shards and fragments all over the kitchen floor. Katie's back was pressed flat against the cold surface of the refrigerator door.

The blood was roaring in her head. She could feel it rush along.

That wasn't the sound of tapping branches. That was the sound of a rather large branch breaking. A branch thick enough that only someone's weight could break it — certainly not the light gusts of wind that were blowing now.

And now someone — or something — was pounding on the window. Fearfully, Katie turned toward the sound of the *THUMP THUMP THUMP*.

Two eyes were glowing outside in the moonlight. They were part of what she realized was a head — no . . . not a head. Just a face. A face suspended in midair — with no body. A face with white glowing eyes, and lips pulled back in a grin to reveal a gleaming row of teeth.

Chapter 30

The eerie headless face continued to grin. It was mouthing words and then screaming something that Katie could barely hear above the rushing roar of blood in her ears. Whatever it was continued to pound on the window.

Wait. If it's pounding, how is it doing it? If it doesn't have a body, where are its hands?

It took Katie a moment to realize that it was Raquelle. Now she could make sense of the words her mouth was screaming.

"For heaven's sake, Katie, wake up and let me in! It's cold out here."

I've gotten so stressed out I'm seeing monsters everywhere, Katie thought. *Even in my best friend's face.*

She ran to the kitchen door and opened it. A chilly gust of air blew in and swirled around Raquelle as she stepped inside. Her cheeks were bright pink.

"Honestly!" Raquelle threw off the black scarf that covered her head and neck with a sweeping flourish. "Where were you — in la-la-land? I rang the bell, I used the doorknocker, I banged on the back door. Then I saw you standing in the kitchen so I pounded on the window. For a while, I thought you were just going to stare at me."

"I guess I was daydreaming, and when I saw you, I didn't recognize you for a minute. You scared me. This house is sort of spooky — so far out in the woods and all. Sometimes I get a little jumpy."

"I'll say." Raquelle hugged herself and gave a little shiver before she removed her coat. "Katie, it's raw out there. Really raw."

So are my nerves, Katie thought.

"Anyway, Katie," Raquelle said as she pulled off her coat, "Maxx isn't coming. He just got a new gig and he asked me if I'd mind if he put in some extra practice time with his drums, so I came on over here. I know I'm a little early — I hope that's okay."

"Sure," Katie said. "C'mon, we'll hang your stuff in the front hall closet."

Katie motioned for Raquelle to follow her. "Even though Maxx can't make it," Katie told her as they walked, "it's a good thing I bought lots of chips since I just broke a bowl of them and they're all over the kitchen floor."

Later, Katie sat on the sofa in front of the TV, nestled in the shelter of Jason's arm. Raquelle sat on the other side of him, taking a sip of soda, her eyes glued to the screen. No one spoke a word. They were watching *Psycho.*

Katie felt her anticpation and fear build as the story unfolded. *I know this so well and yet it scares me just as much each time,* she thought with amazement.

But this is a lot different than the fear I feel when Heath is around me.

She watched as Norman Bates peered at his unsuspecting guest through a hole in the wall at the Bates Motel. She didn't like this part tonight. It reminded her too much of that feeling of being watched.

Jason's arm was around her, and she leaned closer to him and took his hand. He tangled his other hand in her hair and pulled her closer. She felt his lips brush her hair gently.

Then there was a blinding flash of white hot pain that tore through her skull. Katie would have screamed, but she was paralyzed with pain. As she sat there helplessly, Norman Bates stopped spying on his guest.

Now he was talking . . . to Katie.

"Katie," he mouthed, his voice coming out deep, fiery, threatening.

"Katie," he said again, his voice holding her name in a death grip. "You shouldn't be letting him kiss you. You shouldn't be letting him touch you." The voice sneered. "You belong to me. You're my girl — *my special girl.*"

Katie stared in horror. Suddenly the voice wasn't coming from Norman Bates anymore. It was coming from Heath. Heath was there on the screen, surrounded by a fiery halo, his face twisted in rage.

The pain continued to hold Katie paralyzed as Heath continued to threaten, his eyes burning into her soul. "You'd better tell Jason to keep away from MY girl!"

Then Heath's image started to flicker, and the fiery glow began to fade. He no longer bellowed, but the silky whisper he assumed was more insidious — even more threatening.

"Better tell Jason to stay away from my special girl," he cooed gently, the way an adult would whisper to a crying child. "Otherwise, if he's not careful — something bad might happen to him."

Chapter 31

A barely audible sigh of relief escaped Katie's lips as Heath's image faded from the television screen, and the pain faded away with it.

Then she snapped to attention. What about Raquelle and Jason?

But Jason's arm remained relaxed around her shoulders. The room was quiet except for the video. The music was building to a crescendo.

Katie recognized the terrifying sounds, almost like shrieking, that accompanied the shower scene.

Katie turned her head slightly. Out of the corner of her eye she saw Raquelle and Jason gazing at the screen with rapt attention. Raquelle's mouth was open, slightly.

Jason yawned and did a wide stretch.

How can he yawn during a scene like this,

Katie wondered, her radar suddenly on alert. "What's wrong, Jason?"

"Oh — sorry, Katie," Jason smiled, a little sheepishly. "Remember I told you my uncle was coming to visit — the younger one who has that job where he travels a lot? Well, we were up till all hours, talking."

Katie didn't like what she was hearing.

"So then," Jason continued, rubbing at one of his eyes as he talked, "I had to do the early shift at Burger Boy this morning. I had to be in at six A.M. to set everything up."

Katie's eyes were wide with fright.

"You must be dead tired," she blurted out.

She clapped her hand over her mouth. She wished she hadn't said it that way. *Dead tired.*

Jason laughed. "Well, I've been peppier, I admit. But it's no big deal." He flexed his biceps. "See? I'm young and strong."

Raquelle looked away from *Psycho* long enough to say, "Yeah, Katie. He'll be okay. We've all put in an all-nighter or two, and it's not so awful."

You have no idea what awful is, Katie thought, twisting a lock of hair.

"Well, just the same, I think you should drive home with Raquelle," Katie told Jason.

"You're kidding! Raquelle lives in the opposite direction! I'm not taking her out of her way."

"Well, I'll drive you home if you want, Jason," Raquelle said. "But Katie, I think you're overreacting. Besides," Raquelle said with a sidelong glance, "I thought you and Jason would want some time to be alone together."

Normally, Katie would have thought that was true. Now she was torn between wanting him to stay, and wanting him to leave as quickly as possible. To be home, and safe.

"Come on, Katie, calm down." Jason gave her hand a squeeze. "Let's watch the movie."

So Katie prayed everything would be all right, as they sat through *Psycho*. The movie did little to help calm her fears.

After *Psycho* was over, Raquelle left. Then Jason started to pop another video into the VCR. "Just kidding," he said, putting down the cassette. "Let's do something else."

Nothing's going to happen to him, Katie told herself as Jason slid his arms around her. *If only I could make myself believe it*, she thought as he pressed his lips on hers.

While Jason kissed her, Katie nearly lost all thought of her fears.

But later, as they said good-bye, she made sure to tell him to be careful. Twice.

Alone in the house, Katie went through

every room, unplugging all the radios and television sets. She didn't care if anyone who saw what she was doing would think it was strange behavior.

She was too scared.

Chapter 32

Katie blinked as the bright morning sunlight wakened her. For a moment she didn't realize where she was.

Of course, I'm on the couch, she realized instantly as she sat up and looked around. She hadn't wanted to sleep in her own bed. She was too afraid.

Katie pushed a tangle of hair from her forehead. The phone rang so loudly that she jumped.

"Hello?"

"Katie, it's Raquelle."

She didn't have to say another word. The strain in her voice was impossible to miss.

"Is there something wrong with Jason?" Katie asked quickly as she rose to her feet.

"He's had an accident with his car. Katie, he's in the hospital. I just happened to see his parents when I was out running an errand.

They were on their way to see him. They were really upset."

"Tell me everything, Raquelle," Katie whispered. "Will he be all right?"

"He's got a concussion and two broken ribs, but nothing fatal. They said he must've been very lucky or he would've been hurt a lot worse."

Died? Is that what she means? Katie wondered in silent dread. She could feel her heart pounding, and her chest felt tight — constricted.

"How did it happen?" Katie asked, finally. She was afraid that she already *knew*.

"Well, they aren't *exactly* sure, Katie, but he ran the car off the road just in back of your place about half a mile away from your house. He ran head-on into a tree. Katie, I'm so sorry I didn't try to make him ride home with me. I feel so awful, like it's all my fault."

"It's not your fault, Raquelle," Katie told her. *It's probably not even Jason's fault.* "Please, don't blame yourself."

Raquelle's voice trembled. "But Katie, if he hadn't hit the tree, he could have rolled right down the hill. Oh, I wish I hadn't told you that."

Katie thought Raquelle sounded close to tears. "Raquelle, please stop feeling guilty for this."

"I don't know if I can." Raquelle was starting to sob.

"Raquelle, *don't.* Tell me — when you said they didn't know *exactly* how it happened, did they have any ideas at all? Could it have been something wrong with the car — the steering wheel, or the brakes?"

"It wasn't that at all, Katie." Raquelle managed to stop crying. "They think it looks like he fell asleep at the wheel."

Chapter 33

Less than an hour after Raquelle called Katie, they both stood in Jason's hospital room.

"It was incredible — just so weird," Jason said, turning his head slightly to look at Katie.

"Don't strain," she urged. It was obvious that any movement was difficult and painful for Jason. His head, propped up on several pillows, was swathed in bandages, and there were dark sunken circles under his eyes. His face was ashen.

Tubes extended from containers suspended overhead and snaked into his arms, and there was a cast around his chest.

A nurse poked her head in the door. "Five minutes, girls. He's got to get lots of rest." Katie and Raquelle nodded to her and returned to Jason.

"Anyway," he continued staring straight at the ceiling, "as soon as I pulled out of the driveway, I had the strangest feeling. Within an instant, I was totally zonked. I think I conked out before I was too far down the road.

"I'm actually glad I hit the tree, because if I'd continued down the hill, the car could've turned over, and the damage would've been a lot worse."

Jason grimaced suddenly, and clenched his teeth tightly together. Watching him, Katie could almost feel the pain that was shooting through his body. "It only hurts when I breathe," he said when he relaxed.

Katie put her hand on his. "Oh, Jason, this is so unfair," she said softly. She really wanted to cry, but she knew it would only make Jason feel worse.

"My parents are freaking out," he said. "They want all kinds of brain scans and tests. The doctors are going along with some of it, but my doctor keeps telling them I just fell asleep.

"I can't believe it happened, but it's my fault and that's all there is to it."

Katie squeezed his hand. It made her miserable, and enraged that he blamed himself. She believed with all her heart that it wasn't his fault.

Katie shredded the tissue she held in her lap. *What can I do? Heath warned me. Maybe I should've known he'd take matters into his own hands. Perhaps I should have told Jason I didn't want to see him anymore.*

Katie looked at Jason, lying in the hospital bed. He was handsome even now. *The tender line of his mouth told so much about him*, she thought.

I can't give him up. Certainly not for Heath Granger.

There's got to be some way to fight this.

"Do you think I could stay overnight at your house?" Katie asked Raquelle as they drove toward home. "I mean, I know it isn't much notice and I don't mean to put you on the spot . . ."

"Katie, please!" Raquelle said explosively. "You don't even have to ask. Actually — I should have told you — I just *assumed* you wouldn't want to be alone. I've okayed it with my mom already."

"Great." They stopped at Katie's house briefly. Raquelle waited in the car while Katie ran inside and threw some things into a bag. She hurried as fast as she could. Katie didn't like being in the house alone, now. She always had the feeling that Heath's presence was there.

"Monster!" she yelled out before she left.

* * *

Later, they sat in Raquelle's kitchen, sipping cocoa in silence, unable to speak about the tragedy they both knew was in each other's thoughts.

Raquelle's face brightened suddenly as she picked up an opened envelope on the kitchen table. "Katie, with all that's happened, I didn't get a chance to tell you. This is a letter from my sister. She's coming home for a visit soon. Her name's Daphne, and she's graduating from college this year."

Katie blinked as if coming out of a hypnotic trance. "Daphne — like Daphne du Maurier? You don't meet many people with that name."

"Well, my sister's one of a kind," Raquelle chirped. "Wait — I'll show you her picture. She's a knockout."

Raquelle jumped up from the table and ran upstairs. She came back carrying a large book bound in deep maroon leather.

"This is my sister's high school yearbook from when she graduated," Raquelle chattered on, thumbing through the pages.

"There she is — Daphne Martinez."

Katie looked at the picture Raquelle was pointing to. She saw a pretty brown-eyed girl with long dark hair who looked like a more subdued version of Raquelle.

Beside Daphne's picture was a list of her activities — cheerleading, student council, drama club, and homecoming runner-up. "Wow, Raquelle — cheerleading and homecoming runner-up — she must've been pretty popular."

Raquelle sniffed. "Well, *I* think she should've been *queen*." She shrugged. "But the queen was my sister's best friend and she was real nice. I guess I shouldn't mind since Daphne said *she* didn't."

Katie looked back at Daphne's picture for a moment. But then another picture on the page reached out and almost pulled her inside. Katie felt as if a cold wind had just rushed through her soul. She couldn't take her eyes away from what she saw.

At first, Katie couldn't believe the picture was *real*. She couldn't and oh, no, she didn't want to believe . . . that it was HIM.

The guy in the picture looked so neat — dressed in his yearbook best. His hair was so neatly combed and trimmed. He was angled slightly away from the camera. Katie wished the picture had been taken straight on. Also, his chin wasn't as strong as she remembered.

But it was the expression in the eyes and around the lips that made up her mind. *No doubt about it*, she told herself — *that's* him.

Even before she looked underneath the picture she knew the name she would see. And then she looked, and there it was — Heath Granger.

Chapter 34

"Katie! Are you all right?"

Katie heard Raquelle calling to her. The sound was muffled, as if the air around her was too thick to penetrate.

"Katie! You look like you've seen a ghost!"

Katie pressed her hand to her throat.

"I *have*."

She pointed to the picture in the yearbook. "Do you know anything about this guy — Heath Granger?"

Raquelle stared back at her with wide, curious eyes. "Sure, I know all about him. He's kind of a legend. Nobody's told you the story yet?"

Katie shook her head silently. She wondered what he'd done but suspected that whatever it was he was famous for didn't have anything to do with being a hero.

"Good-looking, isn't he?" Raquelle voiced it

as more of a statement than a question. No one would disagree that his looks were exceptional.

"If you could see his *soul*, though," Raquelle went on, "it's probably so ugly you couldn't stand to look at it. He was a horrible person — a *monster*."

Katie nodded, prompting Raquelle to go on.

"Well, it was about four years ago — my sister's senior year — when he showed up. Nobody knew where he came from, and no one ever met his family. He lived alone somewhere, I think."

Katie's face was a taut mask as she listened intently to Raquelle's every word.

"At first, everybody liked him. He was *very* charming, and just seemed to *know* what would make each person like him. He was kind of a rebel, too, and I guess girls who didn't know any better thought that made him more exciting — more romantic."

Katie was glad that Raquelle wasn't looking at her as she could feel her face redden. She knew she had been taken in by Heath's flamboyant manner at the beginning, too. Raquelle was warming to her subject now, enjoying Katie's rapt attention.

"He'd always come roaring up to school on a motorcycle, my sister said. He was so handsome, lots of girls were after him." Raquelle broke off suddenly and looked at Katie. "What made you ask about him like that — out of the blue?"

Katie hesitated. "Just trust me for now Raquelle, please? I have to know everything you can tell me about him."

After a pause where she regarded Katie with a mixture of confusion and curiosity, Raquelle continued. "Well, pretty soon, the *real* Heath Granger started to show. Under that thin, phony veneer of charm, Heath was cold — and mean. He was almost like a — what do you call those people that don't think anything they do is wrong?"

"I think you mean a psychopath." *It would certainly fit the picture perfectly.*

Raquelle nodded. "Yes, that's what he was like — a psychopath. He only wanted to use people, and he didn't care about them at all. He didn't care if he hurt them. He didn't seem to have any *feelings*."

Raquelle shook herself. "I didn't realize how glad I am he's not around anymore. He used to come over here and hang out with my sister's friends all the time — until *that day*."

"*What day?*"

"I'll never forget; he was sitting right on our back porch. The neighbor's cat had had kittens, and I used to go and look at them every day.

They were getting bigger and one of them got big enough to climb the tree in their yard and jump over the fence. It landed on Heath's back."

Raquelle squeezed her eyes shut tight. "Of course, it must've hurt — the kitten was scared and tried to hold on with its claws. But Heath was so furious — he was like a monster. He grabbed the kitten hard, around its neck, and kept shaking it and shaking it. We all yelled at him to stop — but it was like he didn't even hear us. Finally he threw the kitten on the ground — and it didn't move anymore. It was dead."

Raquelle was silent for a moment before she took a deep breath and went on.

"I remember I started crying, and my sister made him leave. She never let him come here again, either. But even though my sister saw right through him, her best friend Cindy didn't."

Raquelle turned the pages of the yearbook. "This is Cindy — the one who was homecoming queen."

Katie looked at the picture and saw a tiny, dark-haired girl whose dancing eyes radiated enthusiasm from her delicate, heart-shaped face. *Poor thing,* she thought. *I know what a miserable time of it you must have had.*

"Heath went after Cindy right away, and no matter what my sister said, Cindy just wouldn't believe it. Of course, Heath just wanted her as a trophy and after he got her he didn't treat her very nicely."

"Were they together very long?"

"Cindy put up with him for a while but then she got fed up — especially with the way he liked to pick on people . . . people who couldn't defend themselves."

Sounds like Heath, all right, Katie said to herself.

"On the night of the prom, Heath showed up dressed like a slob. Then they were in the school parking lot and Heath started picking on Timmy Hensen — a guy who was sort of a nerd, but not a bad guy. Heath picked a fight with Timmy, and got his pants off and ran them up the flagpole — in front of his date and everything. Heath thought it was a big joke."

Katie nodded with understanding.

"Cindy wouldn't go in to the dance with him. She went in by herself and spent the whole night dancing with another guy, Randy Marks. Heath really flew into a rage."

"So, did Heath get into a fight with Randy?"

"No — Randy was a football player. Picking on somebody who could fight back wasn't Heath's style. He spent the night drinking with some friends of his, and the more he drank, the meaner he talked. He said *nobody* dumped him, and he was going to make Cindy understand that . . . *even if he had to kill her.*"

Katie gripped the edge of the table. "Did he hurt her?"

"He wanted to. Some time in the early morning after the dance, Heath got on his motorcycle and roared out toward Cindy's house . . . but he never got there. His motorcycle exploded in flames about a quarter of a mile away. It must have burned for a long time because the body had turned to ashes by the time the accident was discovered."

Katie remembered the strange, smokey smell that Heath sometimes had — the smell that reminded her of fear. Maybe it was more like the smell of death.

"What happened to Cindy?"

"Her family moved away right after that because Cindy kept having such terrible nightmares. She's okay now. She and my sister write to each other."

Terrific, Katie thought. *Now Heath Granger is my nightmare. But how did I get so lucky?*

"Katie!" Raquelle said, suddenly. "I didn't even remember this . . . until now. Cindy lived in your house . . . the one you live in now."

It was only when Raquelle said it that Katie

realized the idea had been in the back of her mind all along. There had to be some connection between her and Cindy — she just knew it.

"Raquelle," Katie asked slowly, "how old was Cindy when she lived in my house?"

Raquelle was thoughtful. "Well — let's see. She lived there all her life, but when they moved she was a junior in high school, like my sister. I think she was . . . seventeen."

Chapter 35

Three nights passed before Heath made a midnight appearance in Katie's dream. She sensed his presence immediately, and hid from him behind the rosebushes at the side of the house. She knew he would find her, but she didn't want to see him a minute before she had to.

"Come out, come out, wherever you are," Heath called in a naughty singsong as he crept through the grass. He lunged suddenly and yanked her arm, pulling her from the shadows.

The sight of him so close made Katie's breath catch in her throat. She had forgotten the piercing intensity of him.

"Somebody might think you weren't glad to see me."

Katie backed away from him. "You hurt Jason! What kind of monster are you?"

"I'm the kind of guy who's a monster if you mess with him," Heath drawled. "I walk tall and play by my own rules," he said with a toss of his head.

"Oh, please. That sounded like a line from a bad movie. What you really are is the kind of guy who wouldn't get caught in a fair fight. Oh, I know who you are. I've seen the yearbook picture."

The bravado disappeared from Heath's face, leaving a blank, stunned expression so full of surprise it was comical.

Well, that wiped the smirk off your face, Katie thought with satisfaction.

"You think you're smart. You think you're so smart . . . but you'll find out you're not," Heath sputtered.

Then he recovered himself and a conniving smile spread itself across his features.

"It doesn't matter that you know anyway, because you see — this is what I'm all about." Heath picked up a medallion that hung around his neck. Katie hadn't noticed it before — it had always hung down inside his shirt. On the face of the medal was a growling animal that looked like a cross between a leopard and a panther.

"You see this? It's just like me — the jungle cat. I'm too slick and too fast and too smooth for you. Because I've got the wits of the jungle cat — and you can't match 'em."

Just look at you strutting and preening, Katie thought. *If you had brains, you'd be dangerous. That's my problem, though. You do have brains — and you* are *dangerous.*

Come on, go ahead and gloat a little bit. Then you'll give me some information. Something I can use. You always let down your guard when you talk about your favorite subject — yourself.

Katie forced herself to hide her feelings of revulsion and amusement. She looked down at the ground.

"I guess I know you're right. You tricked me all along — I have to admit. You're just too smart for me." Katie looked up to gauge Heath's reaction.

If his chest swells any more he'll explode, and my problems will be over.

"It's a good thing you finally realized that, Katie, because this whole thing will be a lot easier if you cooperate. One way or the other — it's going to be done," he said with finality.

"Just exactly what do you mean by 'this whole thing?' "

"Well, it'll be like going to sleep — only we're going to change places. I'll be the one doing the dreaming, and I'll be able to dream myself up."

Heath made a broad sweeping gesture at the surrounding land. "Then I won't have to stick around this dump. I'll be able to go where I want, and I'll get the energy I need from you without having to be a prisoner anymore!"

"What will happen to me? Will I be . . . dead?"

"Oh, no. That wouldn't work at all. I'll have to keep you alive. Let me explain."

Thanks for instructing me on the particulars of the situation, Katie said to herself.

"*You'll* know you're alive, but *they* won't — the doctors and the nurses. That's because the little heart and brain machines won't be able to measure anything. I'll have taken it all for myself . . . almost. I have to leave you *some.*"

Inside, Katie was screaming. In the tone he'd use to give directions, Heath had just as much as told her she'd be buried alive. If everyone thought she was dead, they'd have a funeral. She'd be nailed inside a coffin.

Then she had a thought that was — perhaps — worse. What if she were burned?

"What if I'm cremated, Heath?" Katie shrieked. "Then I'll *really* be dead."

Heath chuckled. "Oh, no, no. Not to worry. You'll be . . . keeping me posted, shall we say? If there is any imminent danger I'll have to let you wake up for a while."

He shook his head. "Wow — I'd like to see their faces when you sit up on the table at the funeral home. What a hoot. They'll think it's a miracle."

Katie fought to control her panic. *If he scares you so much you can't think . . . he's won.*

"What happened to you, Heath? Why are you here? No one could have survived that motorcycle accident — and while you're not alive, you're not — "

"Dead?" Heath finished for her. "No, I'm not dead. It's hard to explain. Did you ever hear the expression 'too mean to die'?"

Chapter 36

Katie wondered how long she'd been staring out the kitchen window. Everything had suddenly come back into focus, and she realized she'd been "somewhere else." She looked down and was surprised to see that she was still holding the towel she'd used to dry the dishes. She knew that the hands holding it were her own, but for a moment they didn't seem connected to her body.

Folding the dish towel carefully, she hung it over the handle of the refrigerator. Katie knew she'd been having episodes like this lately — little lapses.

Yesterday, for example, she had started to take out the trash. She'd been on her way out the back door, trash bag in hand. It had been late afternoon. The first hints of twilight had barely begun.

The next thing Katie knew, it was dark. She was in the same place, the screen door half open, her arm tired from holding the trash bag. She remembered how frightened she'd been . . . and how cold. She had hurried inside and, when she saw the clock, her heart almost stopped. It had been *nine o'clock.*

Katie didn't even feel like she'd been dreaming, that time. But she'd be willing to bet that those lapses had something to do with Heath's plan for taking over her life.

She felt less and less like herself lately. If that meant Heath was getting stronger — as it probably did — she'd have to find a way to get free of him while she could still think clearly.

Calm down, Katie. You can get through this thing. You've got to.

Katie took a deep breath and sat down at the kitchen table. She tried to make a systematic analysis of everything she knew about Heath.

Let's see — he gets very angry when things that would prove his existence are "brought back." He destroys them.

Okay. What else?

Why did he stay away so long after Jason's accident? This was a puzzle. Everything Katie knew about Heath's personality indicated that he'd be eager to gloat about what he'd done — his role in Jason's accident — as soon as he got the chance. But ever since his "TV appearance" he'd stayed away. What was the catch?

One by one, Katie reviewed the times that Heath had made his presence known, other than in dreams. She counted them off on her fingers.

There was the phone call. The time he started the fire. He destroyed his voice on the tape recorder. . . .

Suddenly Katie stopped counting. Her face was lit up with the look of one who has just experienced true insight. She had just been hit with a blinding flash of understanding so clear she could almost see it in front of her.

She knew there was something significant about Heath's failure to show up after he destroyed his taped voice. *He didn't show up in the dream after any of his "appearances" in the waking world.*

Energy — she was sure that was the key. Heath wanted to use her energy to add to his own, to make him stronger. Every time he had to touch the world outside of dreams, he used up energy. Then he had to replenish it before he could come alive again, even in dreams.

Katie's smile grew wider and wider. A plan was already forming in her mind, weaving together as if by itself. She would have to wait until the right moment. If only she could last long enough to use it.

Chapter 37

Katie looked down at Jason, sleeping in his hospital bed. His expression was calm and peaceful — almost serene. She couldn't help thinking . . . *he's so still he almost looks like he's . . .*

Katie fought against the thought. *Stop being ridiculous*, she told herself. *He's not going to die. The nurse told you over and over that his condition wasn't critical. He just needs time — and rest.*

She smoothed the hair on Jason's forehead. "Heath can't get to you here," she whispered.

At least, not yet.

"I'm sorry, Jason," she murmured softly as she continued to stroke his hair.

There was so much she wanted to say to him. If only she could.

Katie walked across the room and pushed

the door gently closed. The bed beside Jason's was empty.

Now Katie was alone with him.

Katie pulled a chair close to Jason's bedside. "If only you could hear me, Jason. I feel like this is all my fault. I should have made you stay away from me."

Why didn't I? I knew the kinds of things Heath is capable of.

She sat back in the chair. "If I can't put a stop to him . . ." her lower lip trembled, "you'll have to stay away from me."

If you can't put a stop to Heath, you won't be around anyway, said a little voice inside her head.

Sitting in the hospital room beside the sleeping Jason, Katie started to cry as she had not cried in a long, long time. Great heaving sobs wracked her body. Her tears fell to the floor, making little, damp puddles.

The horror of the situation was wearing on her terribly, she knew. Her life was a constant battle not to give in to overwhelming terror.

Finally the sobbing stopped. Katie sat quietly for a while, composing herself. She told herself that she mustn't even think of being beaten — not when she had the tiniest spark of life — of herself — left.

Then Katie got up and slowly put on her coat.

"I've got to go, Jason, but I'll see you soon." She thrust out her chin with determination. "You'll see — I'll get rid of Heath. He'll be nothing but a bad dream." She tried to smile. "When this is all over — it'll be just like it never happened. We'll go out all the time and have lots of fun. . . ." She knew she was babbling, and felt her eyes starting to tear again. She fumbled for the door handle.

The feeling that rushed through her body stopped her dead in her tracks. There was a dull throbbing in her head, but the pain was minor compared to the violent nausea that flooded her body.

Katie could almost feel the vomit rising in her throat. She pressed her hands to her throat. Her lips were forcing themselves open — but she wasn't throwing up.

"When this is all over, Jason, we'll ditch her *and have some really wild times!"* Katie put her hand over her mouth, but she couldn't stop the gush of words that issued forth in a deep, rasping voice.

She wanted desperately to run, but she couldn't move. Even if she'd been able to, there was no way she could risk leaving the room. She couldn't let anyone in the hospital hear her talking like this.

Katie struggled to regain control. The feeling of nausea almost made her swoon. The thought that the voice she heard came from inside her own mouth made her sick all over again.

Katie knew that voice. It was Heath's.

"We'll get together and find some real fun chicks. This one's dullsville."

Katie whirled and faced the mirror. For a moment she saw her face, red and contorted. She wore an expression of pure terror.

Then the terror was replaced by something even more frightening. For a horrifying instant Katie wasn't staring at her own reflection any longer. The face that stared back at her from the mirror was Heath Granger's.

"We'll get to be real pals soon, you and me, Jason. I think I can liven you up a bit. We'll have such terrific times you won't even notice that little Miss Goody Two Shoes is gone.

"Well, I'll be seeing you."

Katie felt weak. She leaned against the door and took several deep breaths.

Thank goodness no one had heard her! Her eyes darted around the room. Of course, no one was there; only Jason, who was still sleeping peacefully.

Bending over the side of the sink in Jason's room, Katie rinsed her mouth with soapy water. She would have preferred mouthwash but she didn't mind the soap. Anything was better than the taste of Heath's voice.

She rinsed her mouth again with plain water this time, and finished by drinking a glassful. Then, ever so hesitantly, she raised her eyes to the mirror that hung over the sink.

Her own clear, blue eyes stared back at her. The reflection was of Katie's own face — pale, drained of color — but still her own. She sighed with relief.

It was amazing. She had thought Heath couldn't come up with any terror for her that was worse than what he'd already done. How wrong she was.

He was getting stronger and stronger, she knew.

Katie waited several minutes before leaving the hospital room. She wanted to make sure Heath was gone.

When Katie was absolutely certain it was safe, she stepped out into the hospital corridor. What had happened inside Jason's room seemed even more bizarre in the cold, bright light of the hallway.

Doctors and nurses clad in white strolled or hurried along. Some chatted with each other, looking so relaxed — so normal. Katie was almost afraid to leave all this bright, bustling activity.

As she walked out into the night air and down the front steps, there was only one thought in her mind. *When would Heath be back?*

Chapter 38

The day following Heath's latest appearance, Katie received word that Jason's condition had worsened unexpectedly. He had slipped into a coma.

Though Katie tried to reason that it couldn't possibly be Heath's doing, she couldn't be sure and her state of mind declined sharply. Her nerves were taut, stretched to the limit.

Katie could feel the pressure of Heath's steady, demanding insistence for control. His voice came out of her mouth more and more often and without any warning except for a dizzying sense of impending nausea immediately preceding the incident. Katie herself had no idea what the words would be until she heard them echoing in her ears.

Of course, she knew it was only a matter of time before someone heard the grotesque utterances. Then the day finally arrived.

* * *

Should I go in? Katie wondered as she stood in front of the supermarket. *I always shop here — so all the clerks know me. What if something happens? It would be so embarrassing.*

Katie hesitated, fidgeting from one foot to the other in front of the supermarket. She turned to go away but finally turned again and charged through the door.

That was a mistake.

The incident happened when Katie was in the checkout line. She stood still while the pudgy, round-faced clerk whose name tag said JIMMY counted the bills she'd handed him.

Jimmy was a very careful fellow, Katie remembered. She'd been in his checkout line quite a few times when she'd shopped at the market.

She was watching Jimmy take each bill and turn it so that it faced the same as all the others in the pile. Then he smoothed and straightened each bill before easing it into the drawer. The sudden, sick feeling in her stomach set off a warning bell in Katie's head. She knew what was coming, and she knew it was too late to do anything about it.

"Come on, tubby, give me the change and make it snappy. I haven't got all day to stand

here and watch you diaper dollar bills." The words came out like bone splintering through a meat grinder.

Jimmy looked at Katie as if he'd just seen her head do a 360-degree turn and vomit green slime. She ran out of the supermarket without the groceries or her change.

After that, Katie grew more and more afraid to be around people. She shopped in stores where no one knew her. Each morning as she struggled to open her eyes, her first thought was, *Should I go to school?*

As it happened, the first time Heath "spoke" at school was not nearly so bad as it could have been. It was Raquelle's sense of humor that made the difference.

Katie swore she would never forget that day. She and Raquelle were in the cafeteria. Katie had maneuvered them to a secluded table, claiming she was concerned about Jason and didn't want to have to make small talk with a lot of people. Anyway, it was true.

"Hey pal — pass that mustard over here, huh?" was spoken with Katie's lips, but in Heath's deep, sandpapering tones.

"Wow!" Raquelle nearly spit out a piece of bread in surprise. "That's terrific! Do you do any other voices?"

Katie wanted to hug Raquelle for not acting horrified, or treating her as if she were insane. She wanted to hold on to every minute with Raquelle that day. She knew it might be the last time they had together for a long time — maybe forever.

Soon, Katie knew, the "gag" would wear thin. She didn't "do" any other voices. She couldn't predict what things Heath might say.

Now, Katie decided, was the time to go home, and stay home. She wouldn't be coming back to school again.

Chapter 39

Katie's "lapses" as she called them, were getting longer and more frequent. *Perhaps it's from being alone so much*, she thought.

Since Katie had left school, she had remained at home. She ignored the ringing of the phone or the doorbell fearing what would happen to her voice, or that Heath might "telephone."

Televisions and radios remained disconnected since the night Heath had interrupted *Psycho*. Katie didn't even want to read a book for fear that Heath would leap out from its pages.

Much of the time, though, Katie slept. She couldn't help it. Still, she didn't see Heath in her dreams. *Was he gathering strength for a final challenge?* she wondered.

How much time do I have left?

Outside, tiny buds were forming on trees

and bushes. Spring was on the way. *Will I be around to see it — for real?*

She was staring out the window in her room when she felt the sensation of nausea that always accompanied Heath's vocal outbursts, but this time there was something different. This time there was a roaring sound in her ears — the kind of sound a train makes when it's rushing through a tunnel. Katie was experiencing something she'd never felt before, and the realization brought with it all the terror of the unknown.

Now the roaring sound was fading, growing fainter and fainter until it remained only a whisper in the back of Katie's mind. She was falling; falling into a bottomless pit — and yet standing still at the same time. She fought to regain control, but she knew she was losing.

It's no use, Katie, the thought sounded in her mind. *It won't do you any good. Do I have to explain it to you all over again. Things are going to be different now.*

Heath took a deep breath. *I feel great — never better,* he said to himself. *Pretty soon I can leave this dump out in the sticks for good — get out and cruise some clubs.*

What I ought to do is drop in on some

other dreams — lots of different dreams.

After all, why should a guy like me tie myself down to just one girl?

Then Katie felt herself falling — but falling *up* this time. The roaring noise got louder now, as she was rushing up to meet herself — to become whole again.

Katie hugged herself. She realized she was sitting on the garage floor. Time had passed without her realizing it before — but she had never "woken up" in a different place.

Katie cradled her head in her hands. This was different from having Heath's words come out of her mouth. The words always seemed disconnected from her. She never knew what they would be before she heard them herself.

What had just happened now, in the time between leaving her bedroom and landing here in the garage was much, much worse. Heath's thoughts had been running through Katie's mind.

This is truly the beginning of the end, she knew.

"You're disgusting! Like a leech!" she yelled into the air. Katie picked up a can of motor oil and heaved it as hard as she could. The impact, as it hit the opposite wall of the garage, blew off the top of the can. Motor oil flowed down the cinderblock bricks to form an inky pool on the concrete floor.

Katie wanted to get mad . . . to be furious. As long as she could get mad, her spirit would keep up the will to fight.

But the anger kept slipping away from her — try as she might to hold on. It was hard to stay angry when despair hovered so relentlessly near.

There was still one chance left, Katie told herself. She had a plan — a plan that could work. But she couldn't even try it unless Heath met her in a dream; and not the way he had now, but in a way that she could see him. He had to meet her outside, the way he had for so long. She hadn't had a dream like that, she realized, in quite a while. There was something different about her dreams now. But what?

Wait a minute, Katie thought suddenly. *How did I wind up out here in the garage? If you can't sleepwalk and dream at the same time — what happened?*

Katie tried to think. She didn't really feel as if she'd been dreaming. When she thought really hard about it, she realized that she *could* remember walking downstairs, coming out to the garage — wandering aimlessly.

The eerie truth slammed into her mind as if someone had just held a sign in front of her face. Her dreams had been different lately because she hadn't been dreaming asleep. Katie had been dreaming *awake*.

Chapter 40

Now Katie lost all sense of time. Anyone who looked at her, stretched out on her bed in her rumpled clothes, would have thought she was asleep — nothing more.

Katie had come upstairs hours ago to lie down. She was no longer able to stay on her feet.

For a long time she had drifted in the window of twilight between waking and sleeping, wandering aimlessly through a cottonlike, smoky haze. In the world that gripped her there was no gravity — only a feeling of floating. There was nothing to hold on to — no anchor.

Fragments of dreams were whirling around her like dry leaves caught by gusts of wind and blown in little eddies. Katie became part of several dreams at the same time. Some of the dreams, she realized, weren't her own. Some of the dreams were Heath's.

The dreams whirled faster and faster. Katie's thoughts rolled together with Heath's and whirled along with them. Katie experienced her thoughts and Heath's as if they were TV channels being switched crazily around the dial. Whoever had the remote control was in a manic frenzy.

Through the wild tornado of thoughts and dreams, Katie screamed inside, *This is it! This is it!* The final showdown was taking place.

Katie realized that her thoughts and Heath's were fusing — their minds were becoming less and less separate. Soon there would be one mind — and Heath was fighting for control of it.

In the end, Katie wouldn't really exist.

NO! Katie shouted inside her head. *NONONONONO!*

Katie and Heath locked in a mental tug-of-war. Katie's mind reached out and grabbed the end of the rope and gave a tremendous pull.

It was like being washed to and fro in the ocean. Katie pulled her mind and soul away from Heath, and the tide washed one way. Heath pulled back, and the tide washed the other way.

Katie knew she was winning — for now. She could feel her mind reclaiming itself — thoughts and memories lining up and locking together like pieces of a puzzle. How lon would it last?

Heath had been sapping her mental and emo tional energy for some time now. Katie wa surprised how much she had left. When it cam down to the wire, though, Katie knew she ha the strength — but she didn't have the en durance.

In the end, it was likely that Heath woul win out. But it would be a long, tough fight.

Oh, but he was so impatient. Katie could fee it. He wanted to get away and party on his ow and he wanted it NOW!

As long as he and Katie battled for contro he was confined — a prisoner who could onl wander in her house and the grounds aroun it. He could never go beyond the road wher the accident had blown him into this limbo lan years ago.

I'll make a deal with you, Heath. Come ou and face me.

There was no reply.

I can make it easy for you, Heath, Kati broadcast through her mind. *Maybe you ca win this fight, but it's going to take you a lon time, and you don't like that, do you? You ca hardly wait to get out and infect the world wit your presence. Face me now, and I promise will be a lot quicker.*

Katie sensed that Heath was weighing this idea — considering it. He was coming around. Just a little push and the trap would snap shut. Katie sent another message through her thoughts.

Come on, Heath. You won't have to work so hard. Can't you see how you're struggling? I can keep this up a long time, Heath. A very long time. Haven't you waited long enough already? Aren't you aching?

Meet me on the porch, Heath. Let me be myself for one more hour. One hour — that's all I ask. Then you're free. No more fighting.

It was working. Heath wasn't trying to hold on to Katie's thoughts anymore. He was letting go.

Katie broke free and she was spinning. *It's like riding the tilt-a-whirl at the amusement park*, she thought. *Last chance coming up; one more twirl, hang a right, and go straight on to forever.*

Don't even think of losing.

Chapter 41

When the crazy amusement park ride spun ou Katie landed on a hard, solid surface. *As soli as anything can be in a dream,* she said t herself. It took a while for the dizzy spinnin to calm down enough to focus on anything, bu when it did she realized she was back on th front porch. She had landed on her hands an knees.

Katie could see the skirt of the lacy whit sundress covering her legs. *I really hate th dress,* she said to herself.

She pushed herself up into a standing pos tion and dusted herself off. Then Katie raise her eyes.

"Hello, Heath." He had never looked mor reptilian than he did now, leaning up again the tree in Katie's front yard. She half expecte a forked tongue to dart between his lips whe he opened his mouth to speak.

"Hello, Katie."

Katie thought the words sounded like a hiss. *It's not over till it's over*, she said to herself.

"Thanks for being so — so understanding, Heath. I didn't want to go without having my last few moments all to myself. Of course — I knew you'd win in the end — you're much too clever an opponent for me."

Look at him preening, Katie thought with disgust as she walked toward him. She stared at the medal that hung on the cord around his neck, pretending to be examining it with great care. "It's beautiful," she said finally, looking up at Heath through her eyelashes.

"You know, Heath, I remember how you told me the medal was like you — the image of the jungle cat. How true it is — how true."

Heath's reaction was predictable. He pulled himself up as tall as possible and puffed out his chest. Katie stifled an impulse to giggle.

"Can I see it — the medal? Could you take it off?" Heath looked taken aback. *Please*, Katie prayed.

Then Heath was taking off the medal and handing it to Katie.

For a moment she held it reverently in her hands.

"I want to try it on," Katie said, as if she'd just thought of it. "Let me go inside and see how it looks in the mirror." She was gone be fore Heath could think of an objection.

Inside the house Katie didn't slip the meda around her neck. Holding it firmly in her hand she headed for the back door. Then she slippe out, and into the yard.

Katie headed for the open field behind th house. Beyond it was the main road. It was th road where Heath had had his motorcycle ac cident, years ago. It was the road he couldn' cross.

Katie ran quickly through the yard and soo was wading through the dry, waist-high gras of the field. She kept the house between herse and Heath so that he wouldn't be able to se her until the last minute, when she turned to ward the road.

Still, she'd have to move fast. Heath woul probably get suspicious and wonder why she' been gone so long. Then he'd come after her.

Katie pushed the grass aside as she moved all the while keeping the medal pressed in he hand. She told herself not to look back, bu after a while her need to see how much distanc she'd put between herself and Heath becam too strong.

Katie craned her neck over her right shou der. Heath was quite a ways away, but sh could see him clearly. He was still in the fro ard, but he had moved away from the tree nd was walking toward the side of the house, noving lazily, his hands stuffed in his pockets.

Why, Heath, I'm disappointed in you, Katie aid to herself. *You're not even suspicious yet. 'ou haven't even gone inside to search the ouse.*

I guess you didn't think I'd try to run away. 'ou probably don't think I'd have the nerve.)h, Heath, you just don't know what I've got lanned for you.

At the precise instant Katie was about to tart moving again, Heath looked out toward he field. Their gazes locked.

Oh, no, Katie thought.

She started to move again, as fast as she ould. It was impossible to run. The weeds and rasses grew too thickly at this part of the field.

Katie fought her way forward. A quick back-'ard glance showed that Heath wasn't running fter her. Katie was momentarily confused. *Vhere was he?*

Then she heard the noise, coming closer and loser. Roaring.

Of course, she realized then, Heath wouldn't other chasing after her on foot. He'd come fter her with the motorcycle.

Chapter 42

Katie's lungs strained almost to the burstir point. Sweat poured from her body and h heart hammered in her chest.

The roaring noise filled her ears, growir ever louder as Heath rocketed through th weeds.

Panic seized Katie's heart. She could see th road clearly, only a few yards away. She kne that Heath was gaining on her so quickly no he would reach her before she could reach th road.

The raging noise of the motorcycle told Kat that Heath was close behind her. She turn and saw his face, twisted with madness, ey blazing. He was headed straight for her.

In that instant Katie knew that Heath h gone crazed out of his mind with anger. I wasn't thinking any more — his fury was control.

Heath no longer cared that he still needed Katie's dream to exist. He wasn't going to stop the motorcycle, grab her, and pull her back to the yard. He was going to try to run her down.

The only thing Heath wanted now was to kill her.

The motorcycle was bearing down on Katie — barely three feet away. Acting without thinking, Katie managed to dodge it at the last possible moment, by launching herself into the air and twisting to one side.

Heath couldn't turn the machine fast enough to catch her. Caught off guard, he flew on ahead, barely turning in time to avoid running into the road.

Katie watched him skidding to a frantic stop. *He's still afraid of crossing*, she thought with relief. He had gotten so strong she had wondered about that. She saw Heath maneuver the machine in her direction and realized that she'd lost a lot of ground. Now Heath roared toward her, making her run back toward the house.

After about a quarter of a mile, Katie did a little zigzag turn and was back on course. She could feel herself weakening though, getting worn out, and forced herself to pour every ounce of remaining energy into her mission.

The grass was thinning out now, and Katie was able to run. She threw everything she had into her last desperate, mind-bending, body-breaking steps.

Her feet touched the hard surface of the asphalt road. Heath was behind her on his shining, electric death beetle. He was only inches away.

Katie felt as if the air around her was thick sludge, and everything was happening in slow motion.

MOVE! MOVE! MOVE! she shouted at herself. *You're almost there. You're almost there.*

And then Katie felt herself starting to fall. She saw it all happen as if watching a movie — her foot stepping forward almost by itself, stepping into the hole she saw too late to avoid. She was going down and down, and the ground was rushing up to meet her.

Katie put out her right arm stiffly to brace herself. Somehow she resisted her body's demand that she open her other hand, let go of the medal, and brace herself with her right palm as well.

With a jarring thud, Katie hit the road and rolled, the medal still clutched firmly in her hand. The last thing she saw were the wheels of the motorcycle directly over her face.

Then there was only an orange rush of flame all around her as the motorcycle leapt over the road and landed on the other side. She heard Heath screaming, as if from far away.

An hour passed before Katie realized that her body was still intact, and around another fifteen minutes went by before she realized who she was. *Where am I?* was her next thought.

Katie looked around.

She was in her own room, and she was sitting up in bed. Her nightgown stuck to her body. She felt hot — so hot. She was drenched with sweat.

Suddenly it all came flooding back to her. Heath — the motorcycle — and the flames. *I made it,* she whispered to herself. *I made it, and now I'm going to be all right.*

For the first time, Katie realized the searing, burning pain in her hand. She opened it quickly, and something fell onto the bedspread. Something charred and blackened and round.

Katie stared at it. The cord was almost completely burned away, but on the face of the medal Katie could still make out the scorched image of the jungle cat.

Chapter 43

Dear Diary,

I never saw Heath again after that night h disappeared in flames. I put the medal an what was left of the cord in a little wooden box and I keep it under my bed.

Jason got well. He's coming over tonight.

I didn't lose Jason, or Raquelle, or any o the other friends I'd made when Heath disap peared. I guess that proves they were here fo me all along and not because of any specia powers Heath had.

Raquelle and I are very close — but we neve speak of Heath. I think we both know there ar some things too terrible to speak of, even be tween close friends.

Was Heath just a figment of my imagina tion? Had I actually heard the stories abou the vicious boy whose motorcycle burst int flames and pushed them into the background of my memory, only to weave them into a fantasy of my own making?

I'm sure many people would opt for some sort of explanation like that. Lots of people would find it easy to believe Heath was just the creation of a frightened girl, afraid that she couldn't find out who she was. A girl who was afraid she didn't deserve to have fun and to have friends.

I don't believe that. I was there.

I'm not afraid to go to sleep anymore. But even after all this time, I'm afraid to touch the little wooden box — afraid to shake it to see if there's anything inside that rattles.

Of course, I never open the box to look at what's inside . . . just in case there's nothing there.